TALES OF WAR

TALES OF WAR

BY
LORD DUNSANY

BOSTON
LITTLE, BROWN, AND COMPANY
1918

Norwood Press

Set up and electrotyped by J. S. Cushing Co., Norwood, Mass., U.S.A.

CONTENTS

CONTENTS

I

THE PRAYER OF THE MEN OF DALESWOOD

HE said: "There were only twenty houses in Daleswood. A place you would scarcely have heard of. A village up top of the hills.

"When the war came there was no more than thirty men there between sixteen and forty-five. They all went.

"They all kept together; same battalion, same platoon. They was like that in Daleswood. Used to call the hop pickers foreigners, the ones that come from London. They used to go past Daleswood, some of them, every year, on their way down to the hop fields. Foreigners they used to call them. Kept very much to themselves, did the Daleswood people. Big woods all round them.

1

"Very lucky they was, the Daleswood men. They'd lost no more than five killed and a good sprinkling of wounded. But all the wounded was back again with the platoon. This was up to March when the big offensive started.

"It came very sudden. No bombardment to speak of. Just a burst of Tok Emmas going off all together and lifting the front trench clean out of it; then a barrage behind, and the Boche pouring over in thousands. 'Our luck is holding good,' the Daleswood men said, for their trench wasn't getting it at all. But the platoon on their right got it. And it sounded bad too a long way beyond that. No one could be quite sure. But the platoon on their right was getting it: that was sure enough.

"And then the Boche got through them altogether. A message came to say so. 'How are things on the right?' they said to the runner. 'Bad,' said the runner, and he went back, though Lord knows what he went back to. The Boche was through right enough. 'We'll have to make a defensive flank,' said the platoon commander. He was a Daleswood man too. Came from the big farm. He slipped down a communication trench with a few men, mostly bombers. And they reckoned they wouldn't see any of them any more, for the Boche was on the right, thick as starlings.

"The bullets were snapping over thick to keep them down while the Boche went on, on the right : machine guns, of course. The barrage was screaming well over and dropping far back, and their wire was still all right just in front of them, when they put up a head to look. There was the left platoon of the battalion. One doesn't bother, somehow, so much about another battalion as one's own. One's own gets sort of homely. And there they were wondering how their own officer was getting on, and the few fellows with them, on his defensive flank. The bombs were going off thick. All the Daleswood men were firing half right. It sounded from the noise as if it couldn't last long, as if it would soon be decisive, and the battle be won, or lost, just there on the right, and perhaps the war ended. They didn't notice the left. Nothing to speak of.

"Then a runner came from the left. 'Hullo!' they said, 'How are things over there?'

"'The Boche is through,' he said. 'Where's the officer?' 'Through!' they said. It didn't seem possible. However did he do that? they thought. And the runner went on to the right to look for the officer.

"And then the barrage shifted further back. The shells still screamed over them, but the bursts were further away. That is always a relief. Probably they felt it. But it was bad for all that. Very bad. It meant the Boche was well past them. They realized it after a while.

"They and their bit of wire were somehow just between two waves of attack. Like a bit of stone on the beach with the sea coming in. A platoon was nothing to the Boche; nothing much perhaps just then to anybody. But it was the whole of Daleswood for one long generation.

"The youngest full-grown man they had left behind was fifty, and some one had heard that he had died since the war. There was no one else in Daleswood but women and children, and boys up to seventeen.

"The bombing had stopped on their right; everything was quieter, and the barrage further away. When they began to realize what that meant they began to talk of Daleswood. And then they thought that when all of them were gone there would be nobody who would remember Daleswood just as it used to be. For places alter a little, woods grow, and changes come, trees get cut down, old people die; new houses are built now and then in place of a yew tree, or any old thing, that used to be there before; and one way or another the old things go; and all the

time you have people thinking that the
old times were best, and the old ways
when they were young. And the Daleswood men were beginning to say, 'Who
would there be to remember it just as it
was?'

"There was no gas, the wind being wrong
for it, so they were able to talk, that is if
they shouted, for the bullets alone made
as much noise as breaking up an old shed,
crisper like, more like new timber breaking; and the shells of course was howling
all the time, that is the barrage that was
bursting far back. The trench still stank
of them.

"They said that one of them must go
over and put his hands up, or run away if
he could, whichever he liked, and when the
war was over he would go to some writing
fellow, one of those what makes a living
by it, and tell him all about Daleswood,
just as it used to be, and he would write
it out proper and there it would be for always. They all agreed to that. And then

they talked a bit, as well as they could above that awful screeching, to try and decide who it should be. The eldest, they said, would know Daleswood best. But he said, and they came to agree with him, that it would be a sort of waste to save the life of a man what had had his good time, and they ought to send the youngest, and they would tell him all they knew of Daleswood before his time, and everything would be written down just the same and the old time remembered.

"They had the idea somehow that the women thought more of their own man and their children and the washing and what-not; and that the deep woods and the great hills beyond, and the ploughing and the harvest and snaring rabbits in winter and the sports in the village in summer, and the hundred things that pass the time of one generation in an old, old place like Daleswood, meant less to them than the men. Anyhow they did not quite seem to trust them with the past.

"The youngest of them was only just eighteen. That was Dick. They told him to get out and put his hands up and be quick getting across, as soon as they had told him one or two things about the old time in Daleswood that a youngster like him wouldn't know.

"Well, Dick said he wasn't going, and was making trouble about it, so they told Fred to go. Back, they told him, was best, and come up behind the Boche with his hands up; they would be less likely to shoot when it was back towards their own supports.

"Fred wouldn't go, and so on with the rest. Well, they didn't waste time quarrelling, time being scarce, and they said what was to be done? There was chalk where they were, low down in the trench, a little brown clay on the top of it. There was a great block of it loose near a shelter. They said they would carve with their knives on the big bowlder of chalk all that they knew about Daleswood. They would write where it was and just what it was like, and they would write something of all those little things that pass with a generation. They reckoned on having the time for it. It would take a direct hit with something large, what they call big stuff, to do any harm to that bowlder. They had no confidence in paper, it got so messed up when you were hit; besides, the Boche had been using thermite. Burns, that does.

"They'd one or two men that were handy at carving chalk; used to do the regimental crest and pictures of Hindenburg, and all that. They decided they'd do it in reliefs.

"They started smoothing the chalk. They had nothing more to do but just to think what to write. It was a great big bowlder with plenty of room on it. The Boche seemed not to know that they hadn't killed the Daleswood men, just as the sea mightn't know that one stone stayed dry at the coming in of the tide. A gap between two divisions probably.

"Harry wanted to tell of the woods more than anything. He was afraid they might cut them down because of the war, and no one would know of the larks they had had there as boys. Wonderful old woods they were, with a lot of Spanish chestnut growing low, and tall old oaks over it. Harry wanted them to write down what the foxgloves were like in the wood at the end of summer, standing there in the evening, 'Great solemn rows,' he said, 'all odd in the dusk. All odd in the evening, going there after work; and makes you think of fairies.' There was lots of things about those woods, he said, that ought to be put down if people were to remember Daleswood as it used to be when they knew it. What were the good old days without those woods? he said.

"But another wanted to tell of the time when they cut the hay with scythes, working all those long days at the end of June; there would be no more of that, he said, with machines come in and all.

"There was room to tell of all that and the woods too, said the others, so long as they put it short like.

"And another wanted to tell of the valleys beyond the wood, far afield where the men went working; the women would remember the hay. The great valleys he'd tell of. It was they that made Daleswood. The valleys beyond the wood and the twilight on them in summer. Slopes covered with mint and thyme, all solemn at evening. A hare on them perhaps, sitting as though they were his, then lolloping slowly away. It didn't seem from the way he told of those old valleys that he thought they could ever be to other folk what they were to the Daleswood men in the days he remembered. He spoke of them as though there were something in them, besides the mint and the thyme and the twilight and hares, that would not stay after these men were gone, though he did not say what it was. Scarcely hinted it even.

"And still the Boche did nothing to the Daleswood men. The bullets had ceased altogether. That made it much quieter. The shells still snarled over, bursting far, far away.

"And Bob said tell of Daleswood itself, the old village, with queer chimneys, of red brick, in the wood. There weren't houses like that nowadays. They'd be building new ones and spoiling it, likely, after the war. And that was all he had to say.

"And nobody was for not putting down anything any one said. It was all to go in on the chalk, as much as would go in the time. For they all sort of understood that the Daleswood of what they called the good old time was just the memories that those few men had of the days they had spent there together. And that was the Daleswood they loved, and wanted folks to remember. They were all agreed as to that. And then they said how was they to write it down. And when it came

to writing there was so much to be said,
not spread over a lot of paper I don't
mean, but going down so deep like, that
it seemed to them how their own talk
wouldn't be good enough to say it. And
they knew no other, and didn't know what
to do. I reckon they'd been reading maga-
zines and thought that writing had to be
like that muck. Anyway, they didn't
know what to do. I reckon their talk
would be good enough for Daleswood when
they loved Daleswood like that. But they
didn't, and they were puzzled.

"The Boche was miles away behind them
now, and his barrage with him. Still in
front he did nothing.

"They talked it all over and over, did
the Daleswood men. They tried everything. But somehow or other they couldn't
get near what they wanted to say about
old summer evenings. Time wore on. The
bowlder was smooth and ready, and that
whole generation of Daleswood men could
find no words to say what was in their

hearts about Daleswood. There wasn't time to waste. And the only thing they thought of in the end was 'Please, God, remember Daleswood just like it used to be.' And Bill and Harry carved that on the chalk between them.

"What happened to the Daleswood men? Why, nothing. There come one of them counter-attacks, a regular bastard for Jerry. The French made it and did the Boche in proper. I got the story from a man with a hell of a great big hammer, long afterwards when that trench was well behind our line. He was smashing up a huge great chunk of chalk because he said they all felt it was so damn silly."

II

THE ROAD

THE battery Sergeant-Major was prac-
tically asleep. He was all worn out
by the continuous roar of bombardments
that had been shaking the dugouts and
dazing his brains for weeks. He was pretty
well fed up.

The officer commanding the battery, a
young man in a very neat uniform and of
particularly high birth, came up and spat
in his face. The Sergeant-Major sprang
to attention, received an order, and took
a stick at once and beat up the tired men.
For a message had come to the battery
that some English (God punish them!)
were making a road at X.

The gun was fired. It was one of those
unlucky shots that come on days when
our luck is out. The shell, a 5.9, lit in

the midst of the British working party. It did the Germans little good. It did not stop the deluge of shells that was breaking up their guns and was driving misery down like a wedge into their spirits. It did not improve the temper of the officer commanding the battery, so that the men suffered as acutely as ever under the Sergeant-Major. But it stopped the road for that day.

I seemed to see that road going on in a dream.

Another working party came along next day, with clay pipes and got to work; and next day and the day after. Shells came, but went short or over; the shell holes were neatly patched up; the road went on. Here and there a tree had to be cut, but not often, not many of them were left; it was mostly digging and grubbing up roots, and pushing wheelbarrows along planks and duck-boards, and filling up with stones. Sometimes the engineers would come: that was when streams were crossed.

The engineers made their bridges, and the infantry working party went on with the digging and laying down stones. It was monotonous work. Contours altered, soil altered, even the rock beneath it, but the desolation never; they always worked in desolation and thunder. And so the road went on.

They came to a wide river. They went through a great forest. They passed the ruins of what must have been quite fine towns, big prosperous towns with universities in them. I saw the infantry working party with their stumpy clay pipes, in my dream, a long way on from where that shell had lit, which stopped the road for a day. And behind them curious changes came over the road at X. You saw the infantry going up to the trenches, and going back along it into reserve. They marched at first, but in a few days they were going up in motors, grey busses with shuttered windows. And then the guns came along it, miles and miles of guns,

following after the thunder which was
further off over the hills. And then one
day the cavalry came by. Then stores
in wagons, the thunder muttering further
and further away. I saw farm-carts going
down the road at X. And then one day
all manner of horses and traps and laughing people, farmers and women and boys
all going by to X. There was going to be
a fair.

And far away the road was growing
longer and longer amidst, as always, desolation and thunder. And one day far
away from X the road grew very fine
indeed. It was going proudly through a
mighty city, sweeping in like a river; you
would not think that it ever remembered
duck-boards. There were great palaces
there, with huge armorial eagles blazoned
in stone, and all along each side of the road
was a row of statues of kings. And going
down the road towards the palace, past the
statues of the kings, a tired procession
was riding, full of the flags of the Allies.

And I looked at the flags in my dream, out of national pride to see whether we led, or whether France or America. America went before us, but I could not see the Union Jack in the van, nor the Tricolour either, nor the Stars and Stripes: Belgium led and then Serbia, they that had suffered most.

And before the flags, and before the generals, I saw marching along on foot the ghosts of the working party that were killed at X, gazing about them in admiration as they went, at the great city and at the palaces. And one man, wondering at the Sièges Allée, turned round to the Lance Corporal in charge of the party: "That is a fine road that we made, Frank," he said.

III

AN IMPERIAL MONUMENT

IT is an early summer's morning: the dew is all over France: the train is going eastwards. They are quite slow, those troop trains, and there are few embankments or cuttings in those flat plains, so that you seem to be meandering along through the very life of the people. The roads come right down to the railways, and the sun is shining brightly over the farms and the people going to work along the roads, so that you can see their faces clearly as the slow train passes them by.

They are all women and boys that work on the farms; sometimes perhaps you see a very old man, but nearly always women and boys; they are out working early. They straighten up from their work as we go by and lift their hands to bless us.

We pass by long rows of the tall French poplars, their branches cut away all up the trunk, leaving only an odd round tuft at the top of the tree; but little branches are growing all up the trunk now, and the poplars are looking unkempt. It would be the young men who would cut the branches of the poplars. They would cut them for some useful thrifty purpose that I do not know; and then they would cut them because they were always cut that way, as long ago as the times of the old men's tales about France; but chiefly, I expect, because youth likes to climb difficult trees; that is why they are clipped so very high. And the trunks are all unkempt now.

We go on by many farms with their shapely red-roofed houses; they stand there, having the air of the homes of an ancient people; they would not be out of keeping with any romance that might come, or any romance that has come in the long story of France, and the girls of

those red-roofed houses work all alone in
the fields.

We pass by many willows and come to a
great marsh. In a punt on some open
water an old man is angling. We come to
fields again, and then to a deep wood.
France smiles about us in the open sunlight.

But towards evening we pass over the
border of this pleasant country into a
tragical land of destruction and gloom.
It is not only that murder has walked
here to and fro for years, until all the fields
are ominous with it, but the very fields
themselves have been mutilated until they
are unlike fields, the woods have been
shattered right down to the anemones, and
the houses have been piled in heaps of
rubbish, and the heaps of rubbish have
been scattered by shells. We see no more
trees, no more houses, no more women, no
cattle even now. We have come to the
abomination of desolation. And over it
broods, and will probably brood for ever,
accursed by men and accursed by the very

fields, the hyena-like memory of the Kaiser, who has whitened so many bones.

It may be some satisfaction to his selfishness to know that the monument to it cannot pass away, to know that the shell holes go too deep to be washed away by the healing rains of years, to know that the wasted German generations will not in centuries gather up what has been spilt on the Somme, or France recover in the sunshine of many summers from all the misery that his devilish folly has caused. It is likely to be to such as him a source of satisfaction, for the truly vain care only to be talked of in many mouths; they hysterically love to be thought of, and the notice of mankind is to them a mirror which reflects their futile postures. The admiration of fools they love, and the praise of a slavelike people, but they would sooner be hated by mankind than be ignored and forgotten as is their due. And the truly selfish care only for their imperial selves.

Let us leave him to pass in thought

from ruin to ruin, from wasted field to field, from crater to crater; let us leave his fancy haunting cemeteries in the stricken lands of the world, to find what glee he can in this huge manifestation of his imperial will.

We neither know to what punishment he moves nor can even guess what fitting one is decreed. But the time is surely appointed and the place. Poor trifler with Destiny, who ever had so much to dread?

IV

A WALK TO THE TRENCHES

TO stand at the beginning of a road is always wonderful; for on all roads before they end experience lies, sometimes adventure. And a trench, even as a road, has its beginnings somewhere. In the heart of a very strange country you find them suddenly. A trench may begin in the ruins of a house, may run up out of a ditch; may be cut into a rise of ground sheltered under a hill, and is built in many ways by many men. As to who is the best builder of trenches there can be little doubt, and any British soldier would probably admit that for painstaking work and excellence of construction there are few to rival Von Hindenburg. His Hindenburg line is a model of neatness and comfort, and it would be only a very ungrateful British soldier who would deny it.

You come to the trenches out of strangely wasted lands, you come perhaps to a wood in an agony of contortions, black, branchless, sepulchral trees, and then no more trees at all. The country after that is still called Picardy or Belgium, still has its old name on the map as though it smiled there yet, sheltering cities and hamlet and radiant with orchards and gardens, but the country named Belgium — or whatever it be — is all gone away, and there stretches for miles instead one of the world's great deserts, a thing to take its place no longer with smiling lands, but with Sahara, Gobi, Kalahari, and the Karoo; not to be thought of as Picardy, but more suitably to be named the Desert of Wilhelm. Through these sad lands one goes to come to the trenches. Overhead floats until it is chased away an aëroplane with little black crosses, that you can scarcely see at his respectful height, peering to see what

more harm may be done in the desolation
and ruin. Little flashes sparkle near him,
white puffs spread out round the flashes:
and he goes, and our airmen go away after
him; black puffs break out round our airmen. Up in the sky you hear a faint tap-
tapping. They have got their machine guns
working.

You see many things there that are
unusual in deserts, a good road, a railway,
perhaps a motor bus; you see what was
obviously once a village, and hear English
songs, but no one who has not seen it can
imagine the country in which the trenches
lie, unless he bear a desert clearly in mind,
a desert that has moved from its place on
the map by some enchantment of wizardry,
and come down on a smiling country.
Would it not be glorious to be a Kaiser and
be able to do things like that?

Past all manner of men, past no trees,
no hedges, no fields, but only one field from
skyline to skyline that has been harrowed
by war, one goes with companions that

this event in our history has drawn from all parts of the earth. On that road you may hear all in one walk where is the best place to get lunch in the City; you may hear how they laid a drag for some Irish pack, and what the Master said; you may hear a farmer lamenting over the harm that rhinoceroses do to his coffee crop; you may hear Shakespeare quoted and *La Vie Parisienne*.

In the village you see a lot of German orders, with their silly notes of exclamation after them, written up on notice boards among the ruins. Ruins and German orders. That turning movement of Von Kluck's near Paris in 1914 was a mistake. Had he not done it we might have had ruins and German orders everywhere. And yet Von Kluck may comfort himself with the thought that it is not by his mistakes that Destiny shapes the world: such a nightmare as a world-wide German domination can have had no place amongst the scheme of things.

Beyond the village the batteries are thick. A great howitzer near the road lifts its huge muzzle slowly, fires and goes down again, and lifts again and fires. It is as though Polyphemus had lifted his huge shape slowly, leisurely, from the hillside where he was sitting, and hurled the mountain top, and sat down again. If he is firing pretty regularly you are sure to get the blast of one of them as you go by, and it can be a very strong wind indeed. One's horse, if one is riding, does not very much like it, but I have seen horses far more frightened by a puddle on the road when coming home from hunting in the evening: one 12-inch howitzer more or less in France calls for no great attention from man or beast.

And so we come in sight of the support trenches where we are to dwell for a week before we go on for another mile over the hills, where the black fountains are rising.

V

A WALK IN PICARDY

PICTURE any village you know. In such a village as that the trench begins. That is to say, there are duckboards along a ditch, and the ditch runs into a trench. Only the village is no longer there. It was like some village you know, though perhaps a little merrier, because it was further south and nearer the sun; but it is all gone now. And the trench runs out of the ruins, and is called Windmill Avenue. There must have been a windmill standing there once.

When you come from the ditch to the trench you leave the weeds and soil and trunks of willows and see the bare chalk. At the top of those two white walls is a foot or so of brown clay. The brown clay grows deeper as you come to the hills,

until the chalk has disappeared altogether.
Our alliance with France is new in the
history of man, but it is an old, old union
in the history of the hills. White chalk
with brown clay on top has dipped and
gone under the sea; and the hills of Sussex
and Kent are one with the hills of Picardy.

And so you may pass through the chalk
that lies in that desolate lane with memories
of more silent and happier hills; it all
depends on what the chalk means to you:
you may be unfamiliar with it and in that
case you will not notice it; or you may have
been born among those thyme-scented hills
and yet have no errant fancies, so that you
will not think of the hills that watched
you as a child, but only keep your mind
on the business in hand; that is probably
best.

You come after a while to other trenches:
notice boards guide you, and you keep to
Windmill Avenue. You go by Pear Lane,
Cherry Lane, and Plum Lane. Pear trees,
cherry trees and plum trees must have

grown there. You are passing through
either wild lanes banked with briar, over
which these various trees peered one by
one and showered their blossoms down at
the end of spring, and girls would have
gathered the fruit when it ripened, with
the help of tall young men; or else you are
passing through an old walled garden, and
the pear and the cherry and plum were
growing against the wall, looking south-
wards all through the summer. There is
no way whatever of telling which it was;
it is all one in war; whatever was there is
gone; there remain to-day, and survive,
the names of those three trees only. We
come next to Apple Lane. You must not
think that an apple tree ever grew there,
for we trace here the hand of the wit, who
by naming Plum Lane's neighbour "Apple
Lane" merely commemorates the insepa-
rable connection that plum has with apple
forever in the minds of all who go to
modern war. For by mixing apple with
plum the manufacturer sees the oppor-

tunity of concealing more turnip in the jam, as it were, at the junction of the two forces, than he might be able to do without this unholy alliance.

We come presently to the dens of those who trouble us (but only for our own good), the dugouts of the trench mortar batteries. It is noisy when they push up close to the front line and play for half an hour or so with their rivals: the enemy sends stuff back, our artillery join in; it is as though, while you were playing a game of croquet, giants hundreds of feet high, some of them friendly, some unfriendly, carnivorous and hungry, came and played football on your croquet lawn.

We go on past Battalion Headquarters, and past the dugouts and shelters of various people having business with History, past stores of bombs and the many other ingredients with which history is made, past men coming down who are very hard to pass, for the width of two men and two packs is the width of a communi-

cation trench and sometimes an inch over;
past two men carrying a flying pig slung
on a pole between them; by many turn-
ings; and Windmill Avenue brings you at
last to Company Headquarters in a dugout that Hindenburg made with his German thoroughness.

And there, after a while, descends the
Tok Emma man, the officer commanding
a trench mortar battery, and is given per-
chance a whiskey and water, and sits on
the best empty box that we have to offer,
and lights one of our cigarettes.

"There's going to be a bit of a strafe at
5.30," he says.

VI

WHAT HAPPENED ON THE NIGHT
OF THE TWENTY–SEVENTH

THE night of the twenty-seventh was
Dick Cheeser's first night on sentry.
The night was far gone when he went on
duty; in another hour they would stand to.
Dick Cheeser had camouflaged his age
when he enlisted: he was barely eighteen.
A wonderfully short time ago he was
quite a little boy; now he was in a front-
line trench. It hadn't seemed that things
were going to alter like that. Dick Cheeser
was a ploughboy: long brown furrows
over haughty, magnificent downs seemed
to stretch away into the future as far as
his mind could see. No narrow outlook
either, for the life of nations depends upon
those brown furrows. But there are the
bigger furrows that Mars makes, the long

35

brown trenches of war; the life of nations depends on these too; Dick Cheeser had never pictured these. He had heard talk about a big navy and a lot of Dreadnoughts; silly nonsense he called it. What did one want a big navy for? To keep the Germans out, some people said. But the Germans weren't coming. If they wanted to come, why didn't they come? Anybody could see that they never did come. Some of Dick Cheeser's pals had votes.

And so he had never pictured any change from ploughing the great downs; and here was war at last, and here was he. The Corporal showed him where to stand, told him to keep a good lookout and left him.

And there was Dick Cheeser alone in the dark with an army in front of him, eighty yards away: and, if all tales were true, a pretty horrible army.

The night was awfully still. I use the adverb not as Dick Cheeser would have used it. The stillness awed him. There had

not been a shell all night. He put his head
up over the parapet and waited. Nobody
fired at him. He felt that the night was
waiting for him. He heard voices going
along the trench: some one said it was a
black night: the voices died away. A
mere phrase; the night wasn't black at
all, it was grey. Dick Cheeser was staring at it, and the night was staring back
at him, and seemed to be threatening
him; it was grey, grey as an old cat that
they used to have at home, and as artful.
Yes, thought Dick Cheeser, it was an artful night; that was what was wrong with it.
If shells had come or the Germans, or anything at all, you would know how to take
it; but that quiet mist over huge valleys,
and stillness! Anything might happen.
Dick waited and waited, and the night
waited too. He felt they were watching
each other, the night and he. He felt
that each was crouching. His mind slipped
back to the woods on hills he knew. He
was watching with eyes and ears and

imagination to see what would happen in
No Man's Land under that ominous mist:
but his mind took a peep for all that at
the old woods that he knew. He pictured
himself, he and a band of boys, chasing
squirrels again in the summer. They used
to chase a squirrel from tree to tree,
throwing stones, till they tired it: and
then they might hit it with a stone :
usually not. Sometimes the squirrel would
hide, and a boy would have to climb after
it. It was great sport, thought Dick
Cheeser. What a pity he hadn't had a
catapult in those days, he thought. Somehow the years when he had not had a catapult seemed all to be wasted years. With
a catapult one might get the squirrel almost at once, with luck: and what a
great thing that would be. All the other
boys would come round to look at the
squirrel, and to look at the catapult, and
ask him how he did it. He wouldn't
have to say much, there would be the
squirrel; no boasting would be necessary

with the squirrel lying dead. It might spread to other things, even rabbits; almost anything, in fact. He would certainly get a catapult first thing when he got home. A little wind blew in the night, too cold for summer. It blew away, as it were, the summer of Dick's memories; blew away hills and woods and squirrel. It made for a moment a lane in the mist over No Man's Land. Dick Cheeser peered down it, but it closed again. "No," Night seemed to say, "you don't guess my secret." And the awful hush intensified. "What would they do?" thought the sentry. "What were they planning in all those miles of silence?" Even the Verys were few. When one went up, far hills seemed to sit and brood over the valley: their black shapes seemed to know what would happen in the mist and seemed sworn not to say. The rocket faded, and the hills went back into mystery again, and Dick Cheeser peered level again over the ominous valley.

All the dangers and sinister shapes and evil destinies, lurking between the armies in that mist, that the sentry faced that night cannot be told until the history of the war is written by a historian who can see the mind of the soldier. Not a shell fell all night, no German stirred; Dick Cheeser was relieved at "Stand to" and his comrades stood to beside him, and soon it was wide, golden, welcome dawn.

And for all the threats of night the thing that happened was one that the lonely sentry had never foreseen: in the hour of his watching Dick Cheeser, though scarcely eighteen, became a full-grown man.

VII

STANDING TO

ONE cannot say that one time in the trenches is any more tense than another. One cannot take any one particular hour and call it, in modern nonsensical talk, "typical hour in the trenches." The routine of the trenches has gone on too long for that. The tensest hour ought to be half an hour before dawn, the hour when attacks are expected and men stand to. It is an old convention of war that that is the dangerous hour, the hour when defenders are weakest and attack most to be feared. For darkness favours the attackers then as night favours the lion, and then dawn comes and they can hold their gains in the light. Therefore in every trench in every war the garrison is prepared in that menacing hour, watching in

41

greater numbers than they do the whole night through. As the first lark lifts from meadows they stand there in the dark. Whenever there is any war in any part of the world you may be sure that at that hour men crowd to their parapets: when sleep is deepest in cities they are watching there.

When the dawn shimmers a little, and a grey light comes, and widens, and all of a sudden figures become distinct, and the hour of the attack that is always expected is gone, then perhaps some faint feeling of gladness stirs the newest of the recruits; but chiefly the hour passes like all the other hours there, an unnoticed fragment of the long, long routine that is taken with resignation mingled with jokes.

Dawn comes shy with a wind scarce felt, dawn faint and strangely perceptible, feeble and faint in the east while men still watch the darkness. When did the darkness go? When did the dawn grow golden? It happened as in a moment, a moment you did not see. Guns flash no longer: the sky is gold and serene; dawn stands there like Victory that will shine, on one of these years when the Kaiser goes the way of the older curses of earth. Dawn, and the men unfix bayonets as they step down from the fire-step and clean their rifles with pull-throughs. Not all together, but section by section, for it would not do for a whole company to be caught cleaning their rifles at dawn, or at any other time.

They rub off the mud or the rain that has come at night on their rifles, they detach the magazine and see that its spring is working, they take out the breechblock and oil it, and put back everything clean: and another night is gone; it is one day nearer victory.

VIII

THE SPLENDID TRAVELLER

A TRAVELLER threw his cloak over his shoulder and came down slopes of gold in El Dorado. From incredible heights he came. He came from where the peaks of the pure gold mountain shone a little red with the sunset; from crag to crag of gold he stepped down slowly. Sheer out of romance he came through the golden evening.

It was only an incident of every day; the sun had set or was setting, the air turned chill, and a battalion's bugles were playing "Retreat" when this knightly stranger, a British aëroplane, dipped, and went homeward over the infantry. That beautiful evening call, and the golden cloud bank towering, and that adventurer coming home in the cold, happening all

44

together, revealed in a flash the fact (which hours of thinking sometimes will not bring) that we live in such a period of romance as the troubadours would have envied.

He came, that British airman, over the border, sheer over No Man's Land and the heads of the enemy and the mysterious land behind, snatching the secrets that the enemy would conceal. Either he had defeated the German airmen who would have stopped his going, or they had not dared to try. Who knows what he had done? He had been abroad and was coming home in the evening, as he did every day.

Even when all its romance has been sifted from an age (as the centuries sift) and set apart from the trivial, and when all has been stored by the poets; even then what has any of them more romantic than these adventurers in the evening air, coming home in the twilight with the black shells bursting below?

The infantry look up with the same vague

wonder with which children look at dragon
flies; sometimes they do not look at all,
for all that comes in France has its part
with the wonder of a terrible story as well
as with the incidents of the day, incidents
that recur year in and year out, too often
for us to notice them. If a part of the
moon were to fall off in the sky and come
tumbling to earth, the comment on the
lips of the imperturbable British watchers
that have seen so much would be, "Hullo,
what is Jerry up to now?"

And so the British aëroplane glides home
in the evening, and the light fades from the
air, and what is left of the poplars grows
dark against the sky, and what is left of
the houses grows more mournful in the
gloaming, and night comes, and with it
the sounds of thunder, for the airman has
given his message to the artillery. It is
as though Hermes had gone abroad sailing upon his sandals, and had found some
bad land below those winged feet wherein
men did evil and kept not the laws of gods

or men; and he had brought his message back and the gods were angry.

For the wars we fight to-day are not like other wars, and the wonders of them are unlike other wonders. If we do not see in them the saga and epic, how shall we tell of them?

IX

ENGLAND

"AND then we used to have sausages," said the Sergeant.

"And mashed?" said the Private.

"Yes," said the Sergeant, "and beer. And then we used to go home. It was grand in the evenings. We used to go along a lane that was full of them wild roses. And then we come to the road where the houses were. They all had their bit of a garden, every house."

"Nice, I calls it, a garden," the Private said.

"Yes," said the Sergeant, "they all had their garden. It came right down to the road. Wooden palings: none of that there wire."

"I hates wire," said the Private.

"They didn't have none of it," the

N. C. O. went on. "The gardens came right down to the road, looking lovely. Old Billy Weeks he had them tall pale-blue flowers in his garden nearly as high as a man."

"Hollyhocks?" said the Private.

"No, they wasn't hollyhocks. Lovely they were. We used to stop and look at them, going by every evening. He had a path up the middle of his garden paved with red tiles, Billy Weeks had; and these tall blue flowers growing the whole way along it, both sides like. They was a wonder. Twenty gardens there must have been, counting them all; but none to touch Billy Weeks with his pale-blue flowers. There was an old windmill away to the left. Then there were the swifts sailing by overhead and screeching: just about as high again as the houses. Lord, how them birds did fly. And there was the other young fellows, what were not out walking, standing about by the roadside, just doing nothing at all. One of them

had a flute: Jim Booker, he was. Those
were great days. The bats used to come
out, flutter, flutter, flutter; and then
there'd be a star or two; and the smoke
from the chimneys going all grey; and a
little cold wind going up and down like the
bats; and all the colour going out of things;
and the woods looking all strange, and a
wonderful quiet in them, and a mist coming up from the stream. It's a queer time
that. It's always about that time, the
way I see it: the end of the evening in
the long days, and a star or two, and me
and my girl going home.

"Wouldn't you like to talk about things
for a bit the way you remember them?"

"Oh, no, Sergeant," said the other,
"you go on. You do bring it all back so."

"I used to bring her home," the Sergeant said, "to her father's house. Her
father was keeper there, and they had a
house in the wood. A fine house with
queer old tiles on it, and a lot of large
friendly dogs. I knew them all by name,

same as they knew me. I used to walk home then along the side of the wood. The owls would be about; you could hear them yelling. They'd float out of the wood like, sometimes: all large and white."

"I knows them," said the Private.

"I saw a fox once so close I could nearly touch him, walking like he was on velvet. He just slipped out of the wood."

"Cunning old brute," said the Private.

"That's the time to be out," said the Sergeant. "Ten o'clock on a summer's night, and the night full of noises, not many of them, but what there is, strange, and coming from a great way off, through the quiet, with nothing to stop them. Dogs barking, owls hooting, an old cart; and then just once a sound that you couldn't account for at all, not anyhow. I've heard sounds on nights like that that nobody 'ud think you'd heard, nothing like the flute that young Booker had, nothing like anything on earth."

"I know," said the Private.

"I never told any one before, because they wouldn't believe you. But it doesn't matter now. There'd be a light in the window to guide me when I got home. I'd walk up through the flowers of our garden. We had a lovely garden. Wonderful white and strange the flowers looked of a night-time."

"You bring it all back wonderful," said the Private.

"It's a great thing to have lived," said the Sergeant.

"Yes, Sergeant," said the other, "I wouldn't have missed it, not for anything."

For five days the barrage had rained down behind them: they were utterly cut off and had no hope of rescue: their food was done, and they did not know where they were.

X

SHELLS

WHEN the aëroplanes are home and the sunset has flared away, and it is cold, and night comes down over France, you notice the guns more than you do by day, or else they are actually more active then, I do not know which it is.

. It is then as though a herd of giants, things of enormous height, came out from lairs in the earth and began to play with the hills. It is as though they picked up the tops of the hills in their hands and then let them drop rather slowly. It is exactly like hills falling. You see the flashes all along the sky, and then that lumping thump as though the top of the hill had been let drop, not all in one piece, but crumbled a little as it would drop from your hands if you were three hundred feet high and were fooling about in the night, spoiling what it had taken so long to make. That is heavy stuff bursting, a little way off.

If you are anywhere near a shell that is bursting, you can hear in it a curious metallic ring. That applies to the shells of either side, provided that you are near enough, though usually of course it is the hostile shell and not your own that you are nearest to, and so one distinguishes them. It is curious, after such a colossal event as this explosion must be in the life of a bar of steel, that anything should remain at all of the old bell-like voice of the metal, but it appears to, if you listen attentively; it is perhaps its last remonstrance before leaving its shape and going back to rust in the earth again for ages.

Another of the voices of the night is the whine the shell makes in coming; it is not unlike the cry the hyena utters as soon as it's dark in Africa: "How nice traveller would taste," the hyena seems to say, and

"I want dead White Man." It is the rising note of the shell as it comes nearer, and its dying away when it has gone over, that make it reminiscent of the hyena's method of diction. If it is not going over then it has something quite different to say. It begins the same as the other, it comes up, talking of the back areas with the same long whine as the other. I have heard old hands say "That one is going well over." "Whee-oo,"says the shell; but just where the "oo" should be long drawn out and turn into the hyena's final syllable, it says something quite different. "Zarp," it says. That is bad. Those are the shells that are looking for you.

And then of course there is the whizz-bang coming from close, along his flat trajectory: he has little to say, but comes like a sudden wind, and all that he has to do is done and over at once.

And then there is the gas shell, who goes over gurgling gluttonously, probably in big herds, putting down a barrage. It is

the liquid inside that gurgles before it is
turned to gas by the mild explosion; that
is the explanation of it; yet that does not
prevent one picturing a tribe of cannibals
who have winded some nice juicy men and
are smacking their chops and dribbling in
anticipation.

And a wonderful thing to see, even in
those wonderful nights, is our thermite
bursting over the heads of the Germans.
The shell breaks into a shower of golden
rain; one cannot judge easily at night how
high from the ground it breaks, but about
as high as the tops of trees seen at a hundred yards. It spreads out evenly all
round and rains down slowly; it is a bad
shower to be out in, and for a long time
after it has fallen, the sodden grass of winter,
and the mud and old bones beneath it,
burn quietly in a circle. On such a night
as this, and in such showers, the flying pigs
will go over, which take two men to carry
each of them; they go over and root right
down to the German dugout, where the

German has come in out of the golden rain,
and they fling it all up in the air.

These are such nights as Scheherazade
with all her versatility never dreamed of;
or if such nightmares came she certainly
never told of them, or her august master,
the Sultan, light of the age, would have
had her at once beheaded; and his people
would have deemed that he did well. It
has been reserved for a modern autocrat to
dream such a nightmare, driven to it perhaps by the tales of a white-whiskered
Scheherazade, the Lord of the Kiel Canal;
and being an autocrat he has made the
nightmare a reality for the world. But
the nightmare is stronger than its master,
and grows mightier every night; and the
All-Highest War Lord learns that there are
powers in Hell that are easily summoned
by the rulers of earth, but that go not
easily home.

XI

TWO DEGREES OF ENVY

IT was night in the front line and no
moon, or the moon was hidden.   There
was a strafe going on.   The Tok Emmas
were angry.   And the artillery on both
sides were looking for the Tok Emmas.

Tok Emma, I may explain for the blessed
dwellers in whatever far happy island there
be that has not heard of these things, is the
crude language of Mars.   He has not time
to speak of a trunk mortar battery, for
he is always in a hurry, and so he calls them
T. M.'s.   But Bellona might not hear him
saying T. M., for all the din that she makes:
might think that he said D. N; and so he
calls it Tok Emma.   Ak, Beer, C, Don:
this is the alphabet of Mars.

And the huge minnies were throwing old
limbs out of No Man's Land into the front-

line trench, and shells were rasping down
through the air that seemed to resist them
until it was torn to pieces : they burst and
showers of mud came down from heaven.
Aimlessly, as it seemed, shells were bursting now and then in the air, with a flash
intensely red : the smell of them was drift-
ing down the trenches.

In the middle of all this Bert Butter-
worth was hit. "Only in the foot," his
pals said. "Only !" said Bert. They put
him on a stretcher and carried him down
the trench. They passed Bill Britterling,
standing in the mud, an old friend of Bert's.
Bert's face, twisted with pain, looked up to
Bill for some sympathy.

"Lucky devil," said Bill.

Across the way on the other side of No
Man's Land there was mud the same as
on Bill's side : only the mud over there
stank; it didn't seem to have been kept
clean somehow. And the parapet was
sliding away in places, for working parties
had not had much of a chance. They had

three Tok Emmas working in that battalion front line, and the British batteries
did not quite know where they were, and
there were eight of them looking.

Fritz Groedenschasser, standing in that
unseemly mud, greatly yearned for them
to find soon what they were looking for.
Eight batteries searching for something
they can't find, along a trench in which
you have to be, leaves the elephant hunter's
most desperate tale a little dull and in-
sipid. Not that Fritz Groedenschasser
knew anything about elephant hunting:
he hated all things sporting, and cordially
approved of the execution of Nurse Cavell.
And there was thermite too. Flammen-
werfer was all very well, a good German
weapon: it could burn a man alive at
twenty yards. But this accursed flaming
English thermite could catch you at four
miles. It wasn't fair.

The three German trench mortars were
all still firing. When would the English
batteries find what they were looking for,

and this awful thing stop? The night was cold and smelly.

Fritz shifted his feet in the foul mud, but no warmth came to him that way.

A gust of shells was coming along the trench. Still they had not found the min-newerfer! Fritz moved from his place altogether to see if he could find some place where the parapet was not broken. And as he moved along the sewerlike trench he came on a wooden cross that marked the grave of a man he once had known, now buried some days in the parapet, old Ritz Handelscheiner.

"Lucky devil," said Fritz.

XII

THE MASTER OF NO MAN'S LAND

WHEN the last dynasty has fallen and the last empire passed away, when man himself has gone, there will probably still remain the swede.[1]

There grew a swede in No Man's Land by Croisille near the Somme, and it had grown there for a long while free from man.

It grew as you never saw a swede grow before. It grew tall and strong and weedy. It lifted its green head and gazed round over No Man's Land. Yes, man was gone, and it was the day of the swede.

The storms were tremendous. Sometimes pieces of iron sang through its leaves. But man was gone and it was the day of the swede.

A man used to come there once, a great French farmer, an oppressor of swedes.

[1] The rutabaga or Swedish turnip.

62

Legends were told of him and his herd of cattle, dark traditions that passed down vegetable generations. It was somehow known in those fields that the man ate swedes.

And now his house was gone and he would come no more.

The storms were terrible, but they were better than man. The swede nodded to his companions: the years of freedom had come.

They had always known among them that these years would come. Man had not been there always, but there had always been swedes. He would go some day, suddenly, as he came. That was the faith of the swedes. And when the trees went the swede believed that the day was come. When hundreds of little weeds arrived that were never allowed before, and grew unchecked, he knew it.

After that he grew without any care, in sunlight, moonlight and rain; grew abundantly and luxuriantly in the freedom, and increased in arrogance till he felt himself greater than man. And indeed in those leaden storms that sang often over his foliage all living things seemed equal.

There was little that the Germans left when they retreated from the Somme that was higher than this swede. He grew the tallest thing for miles and miles. He dominated the waste. Two cats slunk by him from a shattered farm: he towered above them contemptuously.

A partridge ran by him once, far, far below his lofty leaves. The night winds mourning in No Man's Land seemed to sing for him alone.

It was surely the hour of the swede. For him, it seemed, was No Man's Land. And there I met him one night by the light of a German rocket and brought him back to our company to cook.

XIII

WEEDS AND WIRE

THINGS had been happening. Divisions were moving. There had been, there was going to be, a stunt. A battalion marched over the hill and sat down by the road. They had left the trenches three days' march to the north and had come to a new country. The officers pulled their maps out; a mild breeze fluttered them; yesterday had been winter and today was spring; but spring in a desolation so complete and far-reaching that you only knew of it by that little wind. It was early March by the calendar, but the wind was blowing out of the gates of April. A platoon commander, feeling that mild wind blowing, forgot his map and began to whistle a tune that suddenly came to him out of the past with the wind. Out of the past it blew and out of the South, a merry vernal tune of a Southern people. Perhaps only one of those that noticed the tune had ever heard it before. An officer sitting near had heard it sung; it reminded him of a holiday long ago in the South.

"Where did you hear that tune?" he asked the platoon commander.

"Oh, the hell of a long way from here," the platoon commander said.

He did not remember quite where it was he had heard it, but he remembered a sunny day in France and a hill all dark with pine woods, and a man coming down at evening out of the woods, and down the slope to the village, singing this song. Between the village and the slope there were orchards in blossom. So that he came with his song for hundreds of yards through orchards. "The hell of a way from here," he said.

For a long while then they sat silent.

"It mightn't have been so very far from here," said the platoon commander. "It

was in France, now I come to think of it.
But it was a lovely part of France, all
woods and orchards. Nothing like this,
thank God." And he glanced with a tired
look at the unutterable desolation.

"Where was it?" said the other.

"In Picardy," he said.

"Aren't we in Picardy now?" said his
friend.

"Are we?" he said.

"I don't know. The maps don't call it
Picardy."

"It was a fine place, anyway," the platoon
commander said. "There seemed always
to be a wonderful light on the hills. A
kind of short grass grew on them, and
it shone in the sun at evening. There
were black woods above them. A man
used to come out of them singing at evening."

He looked wearily round at the brown
desolation of weeds. As far as the two
officers could see there was nothing but
brown weeds and bits of brown barbed

wire. He turned from the desolate scene back to his reminiscences.

"He came singing through the orchards into the village," he said. "A quaint old place with queer gables, called Ville-en-Bois."

"Do you know where we are?" said the other.

"No," said the platoon commander.

"I thought not," he said. "Hadn't you better take a look at the map?"

"I suppose so," said the platoon commander, and he smoothed out his map and wearily got to the business of finding out where he was.

"Good Lord!" he said. "Ville-en-Bois!"

XIV

SPRING IN ENGLAND AND
FLANDERS

VERY soon the earliest primroses will be
coming out in woods wherever they
have been sheltered from the north. They
will grow bolder as the days go by, and
spread and come all down the slopes of sunny
hills. Then the anemones will come, like a
shy pale people, one of the tribes of the elves,
who dare not leave the innermost deeps of
the wood: in those days all the trees will be
in leaf, the bluebells will follow, and certain
fortunate woods will shelter such myriads
of them that the bright fresh green of the
beech trees will flash between two blues, the
blue of the sky and the deeper blue of the
bluebells. Later the violets come, and such
a time as this is the perfect time to see
England: when the cuckoo is heard and he

surprises his hearers; when evenings are
lengthening out and the bat is abroad again;
and all the flowers are out and all the birds
sing. At such a time not only Nature
smiles but our quiet villages and grave old
spires wake up from winter in the mellow
air and wear their centuries lightly. At
such a time you might come just at evening
on one of those old villages in a valley and
find it in the mood to tell you the secret of
the ages that it hid and treasured there
before the Normans came. Who knows?
For they are very old, very wise, very
friendly; they might speak to you one warm
evening. If you went to them after great
suffering they might speak to you; after
nights and nights of shelling over in France,
they might speak to you and you might
hear them clearly.

It would be a long, long story that they
would tell, all about the ages; and it would
vary wonderfully little, much less perhaps
than we think; and the repetitions rambling
on and on in the evening, as the old belfry

spoke and the cottages gathered below it, might sound so soothing after the boom of shells that perhaps you would nearly sleep. And then with one's memory tired out by the war one might never remember the long story they told, when the belfry and the brown-roofed houses all murmured at evening, might never remember even that they had spoken all through that warm spring and evening. We may have heard them speak and forgotten that they have spoken. Who knows? We are at war, and see so many strange things: some we must forget, some we must remember; and we cannot choose which.

To turn from Kent to Flanders is to turn to a time of mourning through all seasons alike. Spring there brings out no leaf on myriad oaks, nor the haze of green that floats like a halo above the heads of the birch trees, that stand with their fairylike trunks haunting the deeps of the woods. For miles and miles and miles summer ripens no crops, leads out no maidens laughing in the moonlight, and brings no harvest home. When Autumn looks on orchards in all that region of mourning he looks upon barren trees that will never blossom again. Winter drives in no sturdy farmers at evening to sit before cheery fires, families meet not at Christmas, and the bells are dumb in belfries; for all by which a man might remember his home has been utterly swept away: has been swept away to make a maniacal dancing ground on which a murderous people dance to their death led by a shallow, clever, callous, imperial clown.

There they dance to their doom till their feet shall find the precipice that was prepared for them on the day that they planned the evil things they have done.

XV

THE NIGHTMARE COUNTRIES

THERE are certain lands in the darker dreams of poetry that stand out in the memory of generations. There is for instance Poe's "Dark tarn of Auber, the ghoul-haunted region of Weir"; there are some queer twists in the river Alph as imagined by Coleridge; two lines of Swinburne:

"By the tideless dolorous inland sea
    In a land of sand and ruin and gold,"
are as haunting as any. There are in literature certain regions of gloom, so splendid that whenever you come on them they leave in the mind a sort of nightmare country which one's thoughts revisit on hearing the lines quoted.

It is pleasant to picture such countries sometimes when sitting before the fire. It

is pleasant because you can banish them by
the closing of a book; a puff of smoke from
a pipe will hide them altogether, and back
come the pleasant, wholesome, familiar
things. But in France they are there
always. In France the nightmare countries
stand all night in the starlight; dawn comes
and they still are there. The dead are
buried out of sight and others take their
places among men; but the lost lands lie
unburied gazing up at the winds; and the
lost woods stand like skeletons all grotesque
in the solitude; the very seasons have fled
from them. The very seasons have fled;
so that if you look up to see whether summer has turned to autumn, or if autumn has
turned to winter yet, nothing remains to
show you. It is like the eccentric dream
of some strange man, very arresting and
mysterious, but lacking certain things that
should be there before you can recognize
it as earthly. It is a mad, mad landscape.
There are miles and miles and miles of it.
It is the biggest thing man has done. It

looks as though man in his pride, with all his clever inventions, had made for himself a sorry attempt at creation.

Indeed when we trace it all back to its origin we find at the beginning of this unhappy story a man who was only an emperor and wished to be something more. He would have ruled the world but has only meddled with it; and his folly has brought misery to millions, and there lies his broken dream on the broken earth. He will never take Paris now. He will never be crowned at Versailles as Emperor of Europe; and after that, most secret dream of all, did not the Cæsars proclaim themselves divine? Was it not whispered among Macedonian courtiers that Alexander was the child of God? And was the Hohenzollern less than these?

What might not force accomplish? All gone now, that dream and the Hohenzollern line broken. A maniacal dream and broken farms all mixed up together: they make a pretty nightmare and the

clouds still gleam at night with the flashes
of shells, and the sky is still troubled by
day with uncouth balloons and the black
bursts of the German shells and the white
of our anti-aircraft.

And below there lies this wonderful waste
land where no girls sing, and where no birds
come but starlings; where no hedgerows
stand, and no lanes with wild roses, and
where no pathways run through fields of
wheat, and there are no fields at all and no
farms and no farmers; and two haystacks
stand on a hill I know, undestroyed in the
desolation, and nobody touches them for
they know the Germans too well; and the
tops have been blown off hills down to the
chalk.   And men say of this place that it is
Pozières and of that place that it is Ginchy;
nothing remains to show that hamlets stood
there at all, and a brown, brown weed grows
over it all for ever; and a mighty spirit has
arisen in man, and no one bows to the War
Lord though many die.   And Liberty is
she who sang her songs of old, and is fair

as she ever was, when men see her in visions, at night in No Man's Land when they have the strength to crawl in : still she walks of a night in Pozières and in Ginchy.

A fanciful man once called himself the Emperor of the Sahara : the German Kaiser has stolen into a fair land and holds with weakening hands a land of craters and weed, and wire and wild cabbages and old German bones.

XVI

SPRING AND THE KAISER

WHILE all the world is waiting for
Spring there lie great spaces in one
of the pleasantest lands to which Spring
cannot come.

Pear trees and cherry and orchards flash
over other lands, blossoming as abundantly
as though their wonder were new, with a
beauty as fresh and surprising as though
nothing like it before had ever adorned
countless centuries. Now with the larch
and soon with the beech trees and hazel, a
bright green blazes forth to illumine the
year. The slopes are covered with violets.
Those who have gardens are beginning to
be proud of them and to point them out
to their neighbours. Almond and peach in
blossom peep over old brick walls. The

land dreams of summer all in the youth of
the year.

But better than all this the Germans
have found war. The simple content of
a people at peace in pleasant countries
counted for nothing with them. Their
Kaiser prepared for war, made speeches
about war, and, when he was ready, made
war. And now the hills that should be
covered with violets are full of murderous
holes, and the holes are half full of empty
meat tins, and the garden walls have gone
and the gardens with them, and there are no
woods left to shelter anemones. Boundless
masses of brown barbed wire straggle over
the landscape. All the orchards there are
cut down out of ruthless spite to hurt France
whom they cannot conquer. All the little
trees that grow near gardens are gone,
aspen, laburnum and lilac. It is like this
for hundreds of miles. Hundreds of ruined
towns gaze at it with vacant windows and
see a land from which even Spring is ban-
ished. And not a ruined house in all the

hundred towns but mourns for some one, man, woman or child; for the Germans make war equally on all in the land where Spring comes no more.

Some day Spring will come back; some day she will shine all April in Picardy again, for Nature is never driven utterly forth, but comes back with her seasons to cover up even the vilest things.

She shall hide the raw earth of the shell holes till the violets come again; she shall bring back even the orchards for Spring to walk in once more; the woods will grow tall again above the southern anemones; and the great abandoned guns of the Germans will rust by the rivers of France. Forgotten like them, the memory of the War Lord will pass with his evil deeds.

XVII

TWO SONGS

OVER slopes of English hills looking south in the time of violets,. evening was falling.

Shadows at edges of woods moved, and then merged in the gloaming.

The bat, like a shadow himself, finding that spring was come, slipped from the dark of the wood as far as a clump of beech trees and fluttered back again on his wonderful quiet wings.

Pairing pigeons were home.

Very young rabbits stole out to gaze at the calm still world. They came out as the stars come. At one time they were not there, and then you saw them, but you did not see them come.

Towering clouds to the west built palaces, cities and mountains; bastions of rose and precipices of gold; giants went home over them draped in mauve by steep rose-pink ravines into emerald-green empires. Turbulences of colour broke out above the departed sun; giants merged into mountains, and cities became seas, and new processions of other fantastic things sailed by. But the chalk slopes facing south smiled on with the same calm light, as though every blade of grass gathered a ray from the gloaming. All the hills faced the evening with that same quiet glow, which faded softly as the air grew colder; and the first star appeared.

Voices came up in the hush, clear from the valley, and ceased. A light was lit, like a spark, in a distant window: more stars appeared and the woods were all dark now, and shapes even on the hill slopes began to grow indistinct.

Home by a laneway in the dim, still evening a girl was going, singing the Marseillaise.

In France where the downs in the north roll away without hedges, as though they were great free giants that man had never confined, as though they were stretching their vast free limbs in the evening, the same light was smiling and glimmering softly away.

A road wound over the downs and away round one of their shoulders. A hush lay over them as though the giants slept, or as though they guarded in silence their ancient, wonderful history.

The stillness deepened and the dimness of twilight; and just before colours fade, while shapes can still be distinguished, there came by the road a farmer leading his Norman horse. High over the horse's withers his collar pointed with brass made him fantastic and huge and strange to see in the evening.

They moved together through that mellow light towards where unseen among the clustered downs the old French farmer's house was sheltered away.

He was going home at evening humming "God Save the King."

XVIII

THE PUNISHMENT

AN exhalation arose, drawn up by the moon, from an old battlefield after the passing of years. It came out of very old craters and gathered from trenches, smoked up from No Man's Land, and the ruins of farms; it rose from the rottenness of dead brigades, and lay for half the night over two armies; but at midnight the moon drew it up all into one phantom and it rose and trailed away eastwards.

It passed over men in grey that were weary of war; it passed over a land once prosperous, happy and mighty, in which were a people that were gradually starving; it passed by ancient belfries in which there were no bells now; it passed over fear and misery and weeping, and so came to the palace at Potsdam. It was the dead of the night between midnight and dawn, and the palace was very still that the Emperor might sleep, and sentries guarded it who made no noise and relieved others in silence. Yet it was not so easy to sleep. Picture to yourself a murderer who had killed a man. Would you sleep? Picture yourself the man that planned this war! Yes, you sleep, but nightmares come.

The phantom entered the chamber. "Come," it said.

The Kaiser leaped up at once as obediently as when he came to attention on parade, years ago, as a subaltern in the Prussian Guard, a man whom no woman or child as yet had ever cursed; he leaped up and followed. They passed the silent sentries; none challenged and none saluted; they were moving swiftly over the town as the felon Gothas go; they came to a cottage in the country. They drifted over a little garden gate, and there in a neat little garden the phantom halted like a wind that has suddenly ceased. "Look," it said.

Should he look ?   Yet he must look.   The
Kaiser looked; and saw a window shining
and a neat room in the cottage : there was
nothing dreadful there; thank the good
German God for that ; it was all right, after
all.   The Kaiser had had a fright, but it
was all right ; there was only a woman with
a baby sitting before the fire, and two
small children and a man.   And it was
quite a jolly room.   And the man was a
young soldier ; and, why, he was a Prussian
Guardsman, — there was his helmet hang-
ing on the wall, — so everything was all
right.   They were jolly German children ;
that was well.   How nice and homely the
room was.   There shone before him, and
showed far off in the night, the visible
reward of German thrift and industry.   It
was all so tidy and neat, and yet they were
quite poor people.   The man had done his
work for the Fatherland, and yet beyond
all that had been able to afford all those
little knickknacks that make a home so
pleasant and that in their humble little

way were luxury. And while the Kaiser
looked the two young children laughed as
they played on the floor, not seeing that
face at the window.

Why! Look at the helmet. That was
lucky. A bullet hole right through the
front of it. That must have gone very
close to the man's head. How ever did it
get through? It must have glanced up-
wards as bullets sometimes do. The hole
was quite low in the helmet. It would be
dreadful to have bullets coming by close
like that. The firelight flickered, and the
lamp shone on, and the children played on
the floor, and the man was smoking out of
a china pipe; he was strong and able and
young, one of the wealth-winners of Germany.

"Have you seen?" said the phantom.

"Yes," said the Kaiser. It was well, he
thought, that a Kaiser should see how his
people lived.

At once the fire went out and the lamp
faded away, the room fell sombrely into

neglect and squalor, and the soldier and the children faded away with the room; all disappeared phantasmally, and nothing remained but the helmet in a kind of glow on the wall, and the woman sitting all by herself in the darkness.

"It has all gone," said the Kaiser.

"It has never been," said the phantom.

The Kaiser looked again. Yes, there was nothing there, it was just a vision. There were the grey walls all damp and uncared for, and that helmet standing out solid and round, like the only real thing among fancies. No, it had never been. It was just a vision.

"It might have been," said the phantom.

Might have been? How might it have been?

"Come," said the phantom.

They drifted away down a little lane that in summer would have had roses, and came to an Uhlan's house; in times of peace a small farmer. Farm buildings in good repair showed even in the night, and the black shapes of haystacks; again a well-kept garden lay by the house.   The phantom and the Kaiser stood in the garden; before them a window glowed in a lamplit room.

"Look," said the phantom.

The Kaiser looked again and saw a young couple; the woman played with a baby, and all was prosperous in the merry room.   Again the hard-won wealth of Germany shone out for all to see, the cosy comfortable furniture spoke of acres well cared for, spoke of victory in the struggle with the seasons on which wealth of nations depends.

"It might have been," said the phantom.

Again the fire died out and the merry scene faded away, leaving a melancholy, ill-kept room, with poverty and mourning haunting dusty corners and the woman sitting alone.

"Why do you show me this?" said the Kaiser.   "Why do you show me these visions?"

"Come," said the phantom.

"What is it?" said the Kaiser. "Where are you bringing me?"

"Come," said the phantom.

They went from window to window, from land to land. You had seen, had you been out that night in Germany, and able to see visions, an imperious figure passing from place to place, looking on many scenes. He looked on them, and families withered away, and happy scenes faded, and the phantom said to him "Come." He expostulated but obeyed; and so they went from window to window of hundreds of farms in Prussia, till they came to the Prussian border and went on into Saxony; and always you would have heard, could you hear spirits speak, "It might have been," "It might have been," repeated from window to window.

They went down through Saxony, heading for Austria. And for long the Kaiser kept that callous, imperious look. But at last he, even he, at last he nearly wept.

And the phantom turned then and swept him back over Saxony, and into Prussia again and over the sentries' heads, back to his comfortable bed where it was so hard to sleep.

And though they had seen thousands of merry homes, homes that can never be merry now, shrines of perpetual mourning; though they had seen thousands of smiling German children, who will never be born now, but were only the visions of hopes blasted by him; for all the leagues over which he had been so ruthlessly hurried, dawn was yet barely breaking.

He had looked on the first few thousand homes of which he had robbed all time, and which he must see with his eyes before he may go hence. The first night of the Kaiser's punishment was accomplished.

XIX

THE ENGLISH SPIRIT

BY the end of the South African war
Sergeant Cane had got one thing
very well fixed in his mind, and that was
that war was an overrated amusement.
He said he "was fed up with it", partly
because that misused metaphor was then
new, partly because every one was saying
it : he felt it right down in his bones, and
he had a long memory. So when wonderful rumours came to the East Anglian
village where he lived, on August 1, 1914,
Sergeant Cane said: "That means war,"
and decided then and there to have nothing
to do with it : it was somebody else's
turn ; he felt he had done enough. Then
came August 4th, and England true to her
destiny, and then Lord Kitchener's appeal
for men. Sergeant Cane had a family to

look after and a nice little house: he had left the army ten years.

In the next week all the men went who had been in the army before, all that were young enough, and a good sprinkling of the young men too who had never been in the army. Men asked Cane if he was going, and he said straight out "No."

By the middle of August Cane was affecting the situation. He was a little rallying point for men who did not want to go. "He knows what it's like," they said.

In the smoking room of the Big House sat the Squire and his son, Arthur Smith; and Sir Munion Boomer-Platt, the Member for the division. The Squire's son had been in the last war as a boy, and like Sergeant Cane had left the army since. All the morning he had been cursing an imaginary general, seated in the War Office at an imaginary desk with Smith's own letter before him, in full view but unopened. Why on earth didn't he answer it, Smith thought. But he was calmer now, and the Squire and Sir Munion were talking of Sergeant Cane.

"Leave him to me," said Sir Munion.

"Very well," said the Squire. So Sir Munion Boomer-Platt went off and called on Sergeant Cane.

Mrs. Cane knew what he had come for.

"Don't let him talk you over, Bill," she said.

"Not he," said Sergeant Cane.

Sir Munion came on Sergeant Cane in his garden.

"A fine day," said Sir Munion. And from that he went on to the war. "If you enlist," he said, "they will make you a sergeant again at once. You will get a sergeant's pay, and your wife will get the new separation allowance."

"Sooner have Cane," said Mrs. Cane.

"Yes, yes, of course," said Sir Munion. "But then there is the medal, probably two or three medals, and the glory of it, and it is such a splendid life."

Sir Munion did warm to a thing whenever he began to hear his own words. He painted war as it has always been painted, one of the most beautiful things you could imagine. And then it mustn't be supposed that it was like those wars that there used to be, a long way off. There would be houses where you would be billeted, and good food, and shady trees and villages wherever you went. And it was such an opportunity of seeing the Continent ("the Continent as it really is," Sir Munion called it) as would never come again, and he only wished he were younger. Sir Munion really did wish it, as he spoke, for his own words stirred him profoundly; but somehow or other they did not stir Sergeant Cane. No, he had done his share, and he had a family to look after.

Sir Munion could not understand him: he went back to the Big House and said so. He had told him all the advantages he could think of that were there to be had for the asking, and Sergeant Cane merely neglected them.

"Let me have a try," said Arthur Smith. "He soldiered with me before."

Sir Munion shrugged his shoulders. He had all the advantages at his fingers' ends, from pay to billeting: there was nothing more to be said. Nevertheless young Smith went.

"Hullo, Sergeant Cane," said Smith.

"Hullo, sir," said the sergeant.

"Do you remember that night at Reit River?"

"Don't I, sir," said Cane.

"One blanket each and no ground sheet?"

"I remember, sir," said Cane.

"Didn't it rain," said Smith.

"It rained that night, proper."

"Drowned a few of the lice, I suppose."

"Not many," said Cane.

"No, not many," Smith reflected. "The Boers had the range all right that time."

"Gave it us proper," said Cane.

"We were hungry that night," said Smith. "I could have eaten biltong."

"I did eat some of it," said Cane. "Not

bad stuff, what there was of it, only not enough."

"I don't think," said Smith, "that I've ever slept on the bare earth since."

"No, sir?" said Cane. "It's hard. You get used to it. But it will always be hard."

"Yes, it will always be hard," said Smith. "Do you remember the time we were thirsty?"

"Oh, yes, sir," said Cane, "I remember that. One doesn't forget that."

"No. I still dream of it sometimes," said Smith. "It makes a nasty dream. I wake with my mouth all dry too, when I dream that."

"Yes," said Cane, "one doesn't forget being thirsty."

"Well," said Smith, "I suppose we're for it all over again?"

"I suppose so, sir," said Cane.

XX

AN INVESTIGATION INTO THE CAUSES AND ORIGIN OF THE WAR

THE German imperial barber has been called up. He must have been called up quite early in the war. I have seen photographs in papers that leave no doubt of that. Who he is I do not know: I once read his name in an article but have forgotten it; few even know if he still lives. And yet what harm he has done! What vast evils he has unwittingly originated! Many years ago he invented a frivolity, a *jeu d'esprit* easily forgivable to an artist in the heyday of his youth, to whom his art was new and even perhaps wonderful. A craft, of course, rather than an art, and a humble craft at that; but then, the man was young, and what will not seem wonderful to youth?

He must have taken the craft very seriously, but as youth takes things seriously, fantastically and with laughter. He must have determined to outshine rivals: he must have gone away and thought, burning candles late perhaps, when all the palace was still. But how can youth think seriously? And there had come to him this absurd, this fantastical conceit. What else would have come? The more seriously he took the tonsorial art, the more he studied its tricks and phrases and heard old barbers lecture, the more sure were the imps of youth to prompt him to laughter and urge him to something outrageous and ridiculous. The background of the dull pomp of Potsdam must have made all this more certain. It was bound to come.

And so one day, or, as I have suggested, suddenly late one night, there came to the young artist bending over tonsorial books that quaint, mad, odd, preposterous inspiration. Ah, what pleasure there is in

the madness of youth; it is not like the
madness of age, clinging to outworn for-
mulæ; it is the madness of breaking away,
of galloping among precipices, of dallying
with the impossible, of courting the absurd.
And this inspiration, it was in none of the
books; the lecturer barbers had not lec-
tured on it, could not dream of it and did
not dare to; there was no tradition for it,
no precedent; it was mad; and to in-
troduce it into the pomp of Potsdam, that
was the daring of madness. And this
preposterous inspiration of the absurd young
barber-madman was nothing less than a
moustache that without any curve at all,
or any suggestion of sanity, should go
suddenly up at the ends very nearly as
high as the eyes!

He must have told his young fellow
craftsmen first, for youth goes first to
youth with its hallucinations. And they,
what could they have said? You cannot
say of madness that it is mad, you cannot
call absurdity absurd. To have criticized

would have revealed jealousy; and as for praise you could not praise a thing like that. They probably shrugged, made gestures; and perhaps one friend warned him. But you cannot warn a man against a madness; if the madness is in possession it will not be warned away: why should it? And then perhaps he went to the old barbers of the Court. You can picture their anger. Age does not learn from youth in any case. But there was the insult to their ancient craft, bad enough if only imagined, but here openly spoken of. And what would come of it? They must have feared, on the one hand, dishonour to their craft if this young barber were treated as his levity deserved; and, on the other hand, could they have feared his success? I think they could not have guessed it.

And then the young idiot with his preposterous inspiration must have looked about to see where he could practise his new absurdity. It should have been enough to have talked about it among his fellow barbers; they would have gone with new zest to their work next day for this delirious interlude, and no harm would have been done. "Fritz," (or Hans) they would have said, "was a bit on last night, a bit full up," or whatever phrase they use to touch on drunkenness; and the thing would have been forgotten. We all have our fancies. But this young fool wanted to get his fancy mixed up with practice: that's where he was mad. And in Potsdam, of all places.

He probably tried his friends first, young barbers at the Court and others of his own standing. None of them were fools enough to be seen going about like that. They had jobs to lose. A Court barber is one thing, a man who cuts ordinary hair is quite another. Why should they become outcasts because their friend chose to be mad?

He probably tried his inferiors then, but they would have been timid folk; they must have seen the thing was absurd, and of course daren't risk it. Again, why should they?

Did he try to get some noble then to patronize his invention? Probably the first refusals he had soon inflamed his madness more, and he threw caution insanely to the winds, and went straight to the Emperor.

It was probably about the time that the Emperor dismissed Bismarck; certainly the drawings of that time show him still with a sane moustache.

The young barber probably chanced on him in this period, finding him bereft of an adviser, and ready to be swayed by whatever whim should come. Perhaps he was attracted by the barber's hardihood, perhaps the absurdity of his inspiration had some fascination for him, perhaps he merely saw that the thing was new and, feeling jaded, let the barber have his way. And so the frivolity became a fact, the absurdity became visible, and honour and riches came the way of the barber.

A small thing, you might say, however

fantastical. And yet I believe the absurdity of that barber to be among the great evils that have brought death nearer to man; whimsical and farcical as it was, yet a thing deadlier than Helen's beauty or Tamerlane's love of skulls. For just as character is outwardly shown so outward things react upon the character; and who, with that daring barber's ludicrous fancy visible always on his face, could quite go the sober way of beneficent monarchs? The fantasy must be mitigated here, set off there; had you such a figure to dress, say for amateur theatricals, you would realize the difficulty. The heavy silver eagle to balance it; the glittering cuirass lower down, preventing the eye from dwelling too long on the barber's absurdity. And then the pose to go with the cuirass and to carry off the wild conceit of that mad, mad barber. He has much to answer for, that eccentric man whose name so few remember. For pose led to actions; and just when Europe most needed a man of wise counsels, restraining the passions of great empires, just then she had ruling over Germany and, unhappily, dominating Austria, a man who every year grew more akin to the folly of that silly barber's youthful inspiration.

Let us forgive the barber. For long I have known from pictures that I have seen of the Kaiser that he has gone to the trenches. Probably he is dead. Let us forgive the barber. But let us bear in mind that the futile fancies of youth may be deadly things, and that one of them falling on a fickle mind may so stir its shallows as to urge it to disturb and set in motion the avalanches of illimitable grief.

XXI

LOST

DESCRIBING a visit, say the papers of March 28th, which the Kaiser paid incognito to Cologne Cathedral on March 18th before the great battle, the Cologne correspondent of the *Tyd* says:

There were only a few persons in the building. Under high arches and in spacious solitude the Kaiser sat, as if in deep thought, before the priests' choir. Behind him his military staff stood respectfully at a distance. Still musing as he rose, the monarch resting both hands on his walking-stick remains standing immovable for some minutes. . . . I shall never forget this picture of the musing monarch praying in Cologne Cathedral on the eve of the great battle.

Probably he won't forget it. The German casualty lists will help to remind him. But what is more to the point is that

this expert propagandist has presumably
received orders that we are not to forget
it, and that the sinister originator of the
then impending holocaust should be toned
down a little in the eyes at least of the
Tyd to something a little more amiable.

And no doubt the little piece of propa-
ganda gave every satisfaction to those who
ordered it, or they would not have passed
it out to the *Tyd*, and the touching little
scene would never have reached our eyes.
At the same time the little tale would have
been better suited to the psychology of
other countries if he had made the War
Lord kneel when he prayed in Cologne
Cathedral, and if he had represented the
Military Staff as standing out of respect
to One who, outside Germany, is held in
greater respect than the All Highest.

And had the War Lord really knelt is
it not possible that he might have found
pity, humility, or even contrition? Things
easily overlooked in so large a cathedral
when sitting erect, as a War Lord, before

the priests' choir, but to be noticed perhaps with one's eyes turned to the ground.

Perhaps he nearly found one of those
things. Perhaps he felt (who knows?)
just for a moment, that in the dimness of
those enormous aisles was something he had
lost a long, long while ago.

One is not mistaken to credit the very
bad with feeling far, faint appeals from
things of glory like Cologne Cathedral;
it is that the appeals come to them too far
and faint on their headlong descent to ruin.

For what was the War Lord seeking?
Did he know that pity for his poor slaugh-
tered people, huddled by him on to our
ceaseless machine guns, might be found by
seeking there? Or was it only that the
lost thing, whatever it was, made that
faint appeal to him, passing the door by
chance, and drew him in, as the scent of
some herb or flower in a moment draws us
back years to look for something lost in
our youth; we gaze back, wondering, and
do not find it.

And to think that perhaps he lost it by very little! That, but for that proud attitude and the respectful staff, he might have seen what was lost, and have come out bringing pity for his people. Might have said to the crowd that gave him that ovation, as we read, outside the door: "My pride has driven you to this needless war, my ambition has made a sacrifice of millions, but it is over, and it shall be no more; I will make no more conquests."

They would have killed him. But for that renunciation, perhaps, however late, the curses of the widows of his people might have kept away from his grave.

But he did not find it. He sat at prayer. Then he stood. Then he marched out: and his staff marched out behind him. And in the gloom of the floor of the vast Cologne Cathedral lie the things that the Kaiser did not find and never will find now. Unnoticed thus, and in some silent moment, passes a man's last chance.

XXII

THE LAST MIRAGE

THE desolation that the German offensive has added to the dominions of
the Kaiser cannot easily be imagined by
any one who has never seen a desert.
Look at it on the map and it is full of the
names of towns and villages; it is in
Europe, where there are no deserts; it is
a fertile province among places of famous
names. Surely it is a proud addition
to an ambitious monarch's possessions.
Surely there is something there that it is
worth while to have conquered at the cost
of army corps. No, nothing. They are
mirage towns. The farms grow Dead Sea
fruit. France recedes before the imperial
clutch. France smiles, but not for him.
His new towns seem to be his because
their names have not yet been removed

from any map, but they crumble at his
approach because France is not for him.
His deadly ambition makes a waste before it as it goes, clutching for cities. It
comes to them and the cities are not there.

I have seen mirages and have heard
others told of, but the best mirages of all
we never hear described; the mirage that
waterless travellers see at the last. Those
fountains rising out of onyx basins, blue
and straight into incredible heights, and
falling and flooding cool white marble;
the haze of spray above their feathery
heads through which the pale green domes
of weathered copper shimmer and shake
a little; mysterious temples, the tombs of
unknown kings; the cataracts coming down
from rose-quartz cliffs, far off but seen
quite clearly, growing to rivers bearing
curious barges to the golden courts of
Sahara. These things we never see; they
are seen at the last by men who die of
thirst.

Even so has the Kaiser looked at the

smiling plains of France. Even so has he
looked on her famous ancient cities and
the farms and the fertile fields and the
woods and orchards of Picardy. With
effort and trouble he has moved towards
them. As he comes near to them the
cities crumble, the woods shrivel and fall,
the farms fade out of Picardy, even the
hedgerows go; it is bare, bare desert.
He had been sure of Paris, he had dreamed
of Versailles and some monstrous corona-
tion, he had thought his insatiable avarice
would be sated. For he had plotted for
conquest of the world, that boundless greed
of his goading him on as a man in the grip
of thirst broods upon lakes.

He sees victory near him now. That
also will fade in the desert of old barbed
wire and weeds. When will he see that
a doom is over all his ambitions? For
his dreams of victory are like those last
dreams that come in deceptive deserts to
dying men.

There is nothing good for him in the

desert of the Somme. Bapaume is not really there, though it be marked on his maps; it is only a wilderness of slates and brick. Peronne looks like a city a long way off, but when you come near it is only the shells of houses. Pozière, Le Sars, Sapigny, are gone altogether.

And all is Dead Sea fruit in a visible desert. The reports of German victories there are mirage like all the rest; they too will fade into weeds and old barbed wire.

And the advances that look like victories, and the ruins that look like cities, and the shell-beaten broken fields that look like farms, — they and the dreams of conquest and all the plots and ambitions, they are all the mirage of a dying dynasty in a desert it made for its doom.

Bones lead up to the desert, bones are scattered about it, it is the most menacing and calamitous waste of all the deadly places that have been inclement to man. It flatters the Hohenzollerns with visions of victory now because they are doomed by it and are about to die. When their race has died the earth shall smile again, for their deadly mirage shall oppress us no more. The cities shall rise again and the farms come back; hedgerows and orchards shall be seen again; the woods shall slowly lift their heads from the dust; and gardens shall come again where the desert was, to bloom in happier ages that forget the Hohenzollerns.

XXIII

A FAMOUS MAN

L AST winter a famous figure walked
in Behagnies. Soldiers came to see
him from their billets all down the Arras
road, from Ervillers and from Sapigny,
and from the ghosts of villages back from
the road, places that once were villages
but are only names now. They would
walk three or four miles, those who could
not get lorries, for his was one of those
names that all men know, not such a name
as a soldier or poet may win, but a name
that *all* men know. They used to go there
at evening.

Four miles away on the left as you went
from Ervillers, the guns mumbled over
the hills, low hills over which the Verys
from the trenches put up their heads and

peered around, — greeny, yellowy heads
that turned the sky sickly, and the clouds
lit up and went grey again all the night
long. As you got near to Behagnies you
lost sight of the Verys, but the guns
mumbled on. A silly little train used to
run on one's left, which used to whistle
loudly, as though it asked to be shelled, but
I never saw a shell coming its way; perhaps
it knew that the German gunners could not
calculate how slow it went. It crossed the
road as you got down to Behagnies.

You passed the graves of two or three
German soldiers with their names on white
wooden crosses, — men killed in 1914; and
then a little cemetery of a French cavalry
regiment, where a big cross stood in the
middle with a wreath and a tricolor badge,
and the names of the men. And then one
saw trees. That was always a wonder,
whether one saw their dark shapes in the
evening, or whether one saw them by day,
and knew from the look of their leaves
whether autumn had come yet, or gone.

In winter at evening one just saw the black bulk of them, but that was no less marvellous than seeing them green in summer; trees by the side of the Arras-Bapaume road, trees in mid-desert in the awful region of Somme. There were not many of them, just a cluster, fewer than the date palms in an oasis in Sahara, but an oasis is an oasis wherever you find it, and a few trees make it. There are little places here and there, few enough as the Arabs know, that the Sahara's deadly sand has never been able to devastate; and there are places even in the Somme that German malice, obeying the Kaiser as the sand of Sahara obeys the accursed sirocco, has not been able to destroy quite to the uttermost. That little cluster of trees at Behagnies is one of these; Divisional Headquarters used to shelter beneath them; and near them was a statue on a lawn which probably stood by the windows of some fine house, though there is no trace of the house but the lawn and that statue now.

And over the way on the left a little further on, just past the officers' club, a large hall stood where one saw that famous figure, whom officers and men alike would come so far to see.

The hall would hold perhaps four or five hundred seats in front of a stage fitted up very simply with red, white and blue cloths, but fitted up by some one that understood the job; and at the back of that stage on those winter evenings walked on his flat and world-renowned feet the figure of Charlie Chaplin.

When aëroplanes came over bombing, the dynamos used to stop for they supplied light to other places besides the cinema, and the shade of Charlie Chaplin would fade away. But the men would wait till the aëroplanes had gone and that famous figure came waddling back to the screen. There he amused tired men newly come from the trenches, there he brought laughter to most of the twelve days that they had out of the line.

He is gone from Behagnies now.   He did
not march in the retreat a little apart
from the troops, with head bent forward and hand thrust in jacket, a flat-
footed Napoleon: yet he is gone; for no
one would have left behind for the enemy
so precious a thing as a Charlie Chaplin
film.   He is gone but he will return.   He
will come with his cane one day along that
Arras road to the old hut in Behagnies;
and men dressed in brown will welcome
him there again.

He will pass beyond it through those
desolate plains, and over the hills beyond
them, beyond Bapaume.   Far hamlets to
the east will know his antics.

And one day surely, in old familiar garb,
without court dress, without removing his
hat, armed with that flexible cane, he will
walk over the faces of the Prussian Guard
and, picking up the Kaiser by the collar,
with infinite nonchalance in finger and
thumb, will place him neatly in a prone
position and solemnly sit on his chest.

XXIV

THE OASES OF DEATH

WHILE the German guns were pounding Amiens and the battle of dull Prussianism against Liberty raged on, they buried Richthofen in the British lines.

They had laid him in a large tent with his broken machine outside it. Thence British airmen carried him to the quiet cemetery, and he was buried among the cypresses in this old resting place of French generations just as though he had come there bringing no harm to France.

Five wreaths were on his coffin, placed there by those who had fought against him up in the air. And under the wreaths on the coffin was spread the German flag.

When the funeral service was over three volleys were fired by the escort, and a hundred aviators paid their last respects to the grave of their greatest enemy; for the chivalry that the Prussians have driven from earth and sea lives on in the blue spaces of the air.

They buried Richthofen at evening, and the planes came droning home as they buried him, and the German guns roared on and guns answered, defending Amiens. And in spite of all, the cemetery had the air of quiet, remaining calm and aloof, as all French graveyards are. For they seem to have no part in the cataclysm that shakes all the world but them; they seem to withdraw amongst memories and to be aloof from time, and, above all, to be quite untroubled by the war that rages to-day, upon which they appear to look out listlessly from among their cypress and yew, and dimly, down a vista of centuries. They are very strange, these little oases of death that remain unmoved and green with their trees still growing, in the midst of a desolation as far as the eye can see, in which cities and villages and trees and hedges and farms and fields and churches are all gone, and where hugely broods a desert. It is as though Death, stalking up and down through France for four years, sparing nothing, had recognized for his own his little gardens, and had spared only them.

XXV

ANGLO–SAXON TYRANNY

"WE need a sea," says Big-Admiral von Tirpitz, "freed of Anglo-Saxon tyranny." Unfortunately neither the British Admiralty nor the American Navy permit us to know how much of the Anglo-Saxon tyranny is done by American destroyers and how much by British ships and even trawlers. It would interest both countries to know, if it could be known. But the Big-Admiral is unjust to France, for the French navy exerts a tyranny at sea that can by no means be overlooked, although naturally from her position in front of the mouth of the Elbe England practises the culminating insupportable tyranny of keeping the High Seas Fleet in the Kiel Canal.

It is not I, but the Big-Admiral, who

chose the word tyranny as descriptive of the activities of the Anglo-Saxon navies. He was making a speech at Dusseldorf on May 25th and was reported in the Dusseldorfer *Nachrichten* on May 27th.

Naturally it does not seem like tyranny to us, even the contrary; but for an admiral, *ein Grosse-Admiral*, lately commanding a High Seas Fleet, it must have been more galling than we perhaps can credit to be confined in a canal. There was he, who should have been breasting the blue, or at any rate doing something salty and nautical, far out in the storms of that sea that the Germans call an Ocean, with the hurricane raging angrily in his whiskers and now and then wafting tufts of them aloft to white the halyards; there was he constrained to a command the duties of which however nobly he did them could be equally well carried out by any respectable bargee. He hoped for a piracy of which the *Lusitania* was merely a beginning; he looked for the bombardment of innumerable towns; he pictured slaughter in many a hamlet of fishermen; he planned more than all those things of which U-boat commanders are guilty; he saw himself a murderous old man, terrible to seafarers, and a scourge of the coasts, and fancied himself chronicled in after years by such as told dark tales of Captain Kidd or the awful buccaneers; but he followed in the end no more desperate courses than to sit and watch his ships on a wharf near Kiel like one of Jacob's night watchmen.

No wonder that what appears to us no more than the necessary protection of women and children in seacoast towns from murder should be to him an intolerable tyranny. No wonder that the guarding of travellers of the allied countries at sea, and even those of the neutrals, should be a most galling thing to the Big-Admiral's thwarted ambition, looking at it from the point of view of one who to white-whiskered age has retained the schoolboy's natural love of the black and yellow flag. A

pirate, he would say, has as much right to
live as wasps or tigers. The Anglo-Saxon
navies, he might argue, have a certain code
of rules for use at sea; they let women get
first into the boats, for instance, when
ships are sinking, and they rescue drown-
ing mariners when they can: no actual
harm in all this, he would feel, though it
would weaken you, as Hindenburg said of
poetry; but if all these little rules are
tyrannously enforced on those who may
think them silly, what is to become of the
pirate? Where, if people like Beattie and
Sims had always had their way, would be
those rollicking tales of the jolly Spanish
Main, and men walking the plank into the
big blue sea, and long, low, rakish craft
putting in to Indian harbours with a cargo
of men and women all hung from the yard-
arm? A melancholy has come over the
spirit of Big-Admiral von Tirpitz in the
years he has spent in the marshes between
the Elbe and Kiel, and in that melancholy
he sees romance crushed; he sees no more

pearl earrings and little gold rings in the hold; he sees British battleships spoiling the Spanish Main, and hateful American cruisers in the old Sargasso Sea; he sees himself, alas, the last of all the pirates.

Let him take comfort. There were always pirates. And in spite of the tyranny of England and America, and of France, which the poor old man perplexed with his troubles forgot, there will be pirates still. Not many perhaps, but enough U-boats will always be able to slip through that tyrannous blockade to spread indiscriminate slaughter amongst the travellers of any nation, enough to hand on the old traditions of murder at sea. And one day Captain Kidd, with such a bow as they used to make in ports of the Spanish Main, will take off his ancient hat, sweeping it low in Hell, and be proud to clasp the hand of the Lord of the Kiel Canal.

XXVI

MEMORIES

> ". . . far-off things
> And battles long ago."

THOSE who live in an old house are necessarily more concerned with paying the plumber, should his art be required, or choosing wall paper that does not clash with the chintzes, than with the traditions that may haunt its corridors. In Ireland,— and no one knows how old that is, for the gods that lived there before the Red Branch came wrote few chronicles on the old grey Irish stones and wrote in their own language, — in Ireland we are more concerned with working it so that Tim Flanagan gets the job he does be looking for.

But in America those who remember Ireland remember her, very often, from old generations; maybe their grandfather migrated, perhaps his grandfather, and Ireland is remembered by old tales treasured among them. Now Tim Flanagan will not be remembered in a year's time when he has the job for which he has got us to agitate, and the jobberies that stir us move not the pen of History.

But the tales that Irish generations hand down beyond the Atlantic have to be tales that are worth remembering. They are tales that have to stand the supreme test, tales that a child will listen to by the fireside of an evening, so that they go down with those early remembered evenings that are last of all to go of the memories of a lifetime. A tale that a child will listen to must have much grandeur. Any cheap stuff will do for us, bad journalism, and novels by girls that could get no other jobs; but a child looks for those things in a tale that are simple and noble and epic, the things that Earth remembers. And so they tell, over there, tales of Sarsfield and of the old Irish Brigade; they tell, of an evening, of Owen Roe O'Neill. And into those tales come the plains of Flanders again and the ancient towns of France, towns famous long ago and famous yet: let us rather think of them as famous names and not as the sad ruins we have seen, melancholy by day and monstrous in the moonlight.

Many an Irishman who sails from America for those historic lands knows that the old trees that stand there have their roots far down in soil once richened by Irish blood. When the Boyne was lost and won, and Ireland had lost her King, many an Irishman with all his wealth in a scabbard looked upon exile as his sovereign's court. And so they came to the lands of foreign kings, with nothing to offer for the hospitality that was given them but a sword; and it usually was a sword with which kings were well content. Louis XV had many of them, and was glad to have them at Fontenoy; the Spanish King admitted them to the Golden Fleece; they defended

Maria Theresa. Landen in Flanders and
Cremona knew them. A volume were
needed to tell of all those swords; more
than one Muse has remembered them. It
was not disloyalty that drove them forth;
their King was gone, they followed, the
oak was smitten and brown were the leaves
of the tree.

But no such mournful metaphor applies
to the men who march to-day towards the
plains where the "Wild Geese" were driven.
They go with no country mourning them,
but their whole land cheers them on; they
go to the inherited battlefields. And there
is this difference in their attitude to kings,
that those knightly Irishmen of old, driven
homeless over-sea, appeared as exiles sup-
pliant for shelter before the face of the
Grand Monarch, and he, no doubt with
exquisite French grace, gave back to them
all they had lost except what was lost forever, salving so far as he could the in-
justice suffered by each. But to-day when
might, for its turn, is in the hands of de-

mocracies, the men whose fathers built the Statue of Liberty have left their country to bring back an exiled king to his home, and to right what can be righted of the ghastly wrongs of Flanders.

And if men's prayers are heard, as many say, old saints will hear old supplications going up by starlight with a certain wistful, musical intonation that has linked the towns of Limerick and Cork with the fields of Flanders before.

XXVII

THE MOVEMENT

FOR many years Eliphaz Griggs was comparatively silent. Not that he did not talk on all occasions whenever he could find hearers, he did that at great length; but for many years he addressed no public meeting, and was no part of the normal life of the northeast end of Hyde Park or Trafalgar Square. And then one day he was talking in a public house where he had gone to talk on the only subject that was dear to him. He waited, as was his custom, until five or six men were present, and then he began. "Ye're all damned, I'm saying, damned from the day you were born. Your portion is Tophet."

And on that day there happened what had never happened in his experience be-

fore.   Men used to listen in a tolerant way,
and say little over their beer, for that is the
English custom;   and that would be all.
But to-day a man rose up with flashing
eyes and went over to Eliphaz and gripped
him by the hand: "They're *all* damned,"
said the stranger.

That was the turning point in the life
of Eliphaz.   Up to that moment he had
been a lonely crank, and men thought he
was queer;   but now there were two of
them and he became a Movement.   A
Movement in England may do what it
likes: there was a Movement, before the
War, for spoiling tulips in Kew Gardens
and breaking church windows;   it had its
run like the rest.

The name of Eliphaz's new friend was
Ezekiel Pim: and they drew up rules for
their Movement almost at once;   and very
soon country inns knew Eliphaz no more.
And for some while they missed him where
he used to drop in of an evening to tell them
they were all damned;   and then a man

proved one day that the earth was flat, and they all forgot Eliphaz.

But Eliphaz went to Hyde Park and Ezekiel Pim went with him, and there you would see them close to the Marble Arch on any fine Sunday afternoon, preaching their Movement to the people of London. "You are all damned," said Eliphaz. "Your portion shall be damnation for everlasting."

"*All* damned," added Ezekiel.

Eliphaz was the orator. He would picture Hell to you as it really is. He made you see pretty much what it will be like to wriggle and turn and squirm, and never escape from burning. But Ezekiel Pim, though he seldom said more than three words, uttered those words with such alarming sincerity and had such a sure conviction shining in his eyes that searched right in your face as he said them, and his long hair waved so weirdly as his head shot forward when he said "You're *all* damned", that Ezekiel Pim brought home to you that the vivid descriptions of Eliphaz really applied to *you*.

People who lead bad lives get their sensibilities hardened. These did not care very much what Eliphaz said. But girls at school, and several governesses, and even some young clergy, were very much affected. Eliphaz Griggs and Ezekiel Pim seemed to bring Hell so near to you. You could almost feel it baking the Marble Arch from two to four on Sundays. And at four o'clock the Surbiton Branch of the International Anarchists used to come along, and Eliphaz Griggs and Ezekiel Pim would pack up their flag and go, for the pitch belonged to the Surbiton people till six; and the crank Movements punctiliously recognize each other's rights. If they fought among themselves, which is quite unthinkable, the police would run them in; it is the one thing that an anarchist in England may never do.

When the War came the two speakers doubled their efforts. The way they looked at it was that here was a counter-attraction taking people's minds off the subject of their own damnation just as they had got them to think about it. Eliphaz worked as he had never worked before; he spared nobody; but it was still Ezekiel Pim who somehow brought it most home to them.

One fine spring afternoon Eliphaz Griggs was speaking at his usual place and time; he had wound himself up wonderfully. "You are damned," he was saying, "for ever and ever and ever. Your sins have found you out. Your filthy lives will be as fuel round you and shall burn for ever and ever."

"Look here," said a Canadian soldier in the crowd, "we shouldn't allow that in Ottawa."

"What?" asked an English girl.

"Why, telling us we're all damned like that," he said.

"Oh, this is England," she said. "They may all say what they like here."

"You are all damned," said Ezekiel,

jerking forward his head and shoulders till his hair flapped out behind. "*All, all, all* damned."

"I'm damned if I am," said the Canadian soldier.

"Ah," said Ezekiel, and a sly look came into his face.

Eliphaz flamed on. "Your sins are remembered. Satan shall grin at you. He shall heap cinders on you for ever and ever. Woe to you, filthy livers. Woe to you, sinners. Hell is your portion. There shall be none to grieve for you. You shall dwell in torment for ages. None shall be spared, not one. Woe everlasting . . . . Oh, I beg pardon, gentlemen, I'm sure." For the Pacifists' League had been kept waiting three minutes. It was their turn to-day at four.

XXVIII

NATURE'S CAD

THE claim of Professor Grotius Jan Beek to have discovered, or learned, the language of the greater apes has been demonstrated clearly enough. He is not the original discoverer of the fact that they have what may be said to correspond with a language; nor is he the first man to have lived for some while in the jungle protected by wooden bars, with a view to acquiring some knowledge of the meaning of the various syllables that gorillas appear to utter. If so crude a collection of sounds, amounting to less than a hundred words, if words they are, may be called a language, it may be admitted that the Professor has learned it, as his recent experiments show. What he has not proved is his assertion that he has actually conversed with a

139

gorilla, or by signs, or grunts, or any means whatever obtained an insight, as he put it, into its mentality, or, as we should put it, its point of view. This Professor Beek claims to have done; and though he gives us a certain plausible corroboration of a kind which makes his story appear likely, it should be borne in mind that it is not of the nature of proof.

The Professor's story is briefly that having acquired this language, which nobody that has witnessed his experiments will call in question, he went back to the jungle for a week, living all the time in the ordinary explorer's cage of the Blik pattern. Towards the very end of the week a big male gorilla came by, and the Professor attracted it by the one word "Food." It came, he says, close to the cage, and seemed prepared to talk but became very angry on seeing a man there, and beat the cage and would say nothing. The Professor says that he asked it why it was angry. He admits that he had learned no more than

forty words of this language, but believes
that there are perhaps thirty more. Much
however is expressed, as he says, by mere
intonation.   Anger, for instance; and
scores of allied words, such as terrible,
frightful, kill, whether noun, verb or ad-
jective, are expressed, he says, by a mere
growl. Nor is there any word for "Why ",
but queries are signified by the inflexion
of the voice.

When he asked it why it was angry the
gorilla said that men killed him, and added
a noise that the professor said was evidently meant to allude to guns. The only
word used, he says, in this remark of the
gorilla's was the word that signified "man."
The sentence as understood by the professor amounted to "Man kill me. Guns."
But the word "kill" was represented simply
by a snarl, "me" by slapping its chest, and
"guns" as I have explained was only represented by a noise. The Professor believes
that ultimately a word for guns may be
evolved out of that noise, but thinks that

it will take many centuries, and that if during that time guns should cease to be in use, this stimulus being withdrawn, the word will never be evolved at all, nor of course will it be needed.

The Professor tried, by evincing interest, ignorance, and incredulity, and even indignation, to encourage the gorilla to say more; but to his disappointment, all the more intense after having exchanged that one word of conversation with one of the beasts, the gorilla only repeated what it had said, and beat on the cage again. For half an hour this went on, the Professor showing every sign of sympathy, the gorilla raging and beating upon the cage.

It was half an hour of the most intense excitement to the Professor, during which time he saw the realization of dreams that many considered crazy, glittering as it were within his grasp, and all the while this ridiculous gorilla would do nothing but repeat the mere shred of a sentence and beat the cage with its great hands; and the heat of course was intense. And by the end of the half hour the excitement and the heat seem to have got the better of the Professor's temper, and he waved the 'disgusting brute angrily away with a gesture that probably was not much less impatient than the gorilla's own. And at that the animal suddenly became voluble. He beat more furiously than ever upon the cage and slipped his great fingers through the bars, trying to reach the Professor, and poured out volumes of ape-chatter.

Why, why did men shoot at him, he asked. He made himself terrible, therefore men ought to love him. That was the whole burden of what the Professor calls its argument. "Me, me terrible," two slaps on the chest and then a growl. "Man love me." And then the emphatic negative word, and the sound that meant guns, and sudden furious rushes at the cage to try to get at the Professor.

The gorilla, Professor Beek explains, evidently admired only strength; when-

ever he said "I make myself terrible to
Man," a sentence he often repeated, he
drew himself up and thrust out his huge
chest and bared his frightful teeth; and
certainly, the Professor says, there was
something terribly grand about the menacing brute. "Me terrible," he repeated
again and again, "Me terrible. Sky, sun,
stars with me. Man love me. Man love
me. No?" It meant that all the great
forces of nature assisted him and his terrible
teeth, which he gnashed repeatedly, and
that therefore man should love him, and
he opened his great jaws wide as he said
this, showing all the brutal force of them.

There was to my mind a genuine ring in
Professor Beek's story, because he was
obviously so much more concerned, and
really troubled, by the dreadful depravity
of this animal's point of view, or mentality
as he called it, than he was concerned with
whether or not we believed what he had
said.

And I mentioned that there was a circumstance in his story of a plausible and even corroborative nature.   It is this. Professor Beek, who noticed at the time a bullet wound in the tip of the gorilla's left ear, by means of which it was luckily identified, put his analysis of its mentality in writing and showed it to several others, before he had any way of accounting for the beast having such a mind.

Long afterwards it was definitely ascertained that this animal had been caught when young on the slopes of Kilimanjaro and trained and even educated, so far as such things are possible, by an eminent German Professor, a *persona grata* at the Court of Berlin.

XXIX

THE HOME OF HERR SCHNITZEL-
HAASER

THE guns in the town of Greinstein
were faintly audible. The family of
Schnitzelhaaser lived alone there in mourning, an old man and old woman. They
never went out or saw any one, for they
knew they could not speak as though they
did not mourn. They feared that their
secret would escape them. They had never
cared for the war that the War Lord made.
They no longer cared what he did with it.
They never read his speeches; they never
hung out flags when he ordered flags: they
hadn't the heart to.

They had had four sons.

The lonely old couple would go as far as
the shop for food. Hunger stalked behind
them. They just beat hunger every day,

and so saw evening : but there was nothing
to spare. Otherwise they did not go out
at all. Hunger had been coming slowly
nearer of late. They had nothing but the
ration, and the ration was growing smaller.
They had one pig of their own, but the law
said you might not kill it. So the pig was
no good to them.

They used to go and look at that pig
sometimes when hunger pinched. But
more than that they did not dare to con-
template.

Hunger came nearer and nearer. The
war was going to end by the first of July.
The War Lord was going to take Paris on
this day and that would end the war at
once. But then the war was always going
to end. It was going to end in 1914, and
their four sons were to have come home
when the leaves fell. The War Lord had
promised that. And even if it did end, that
would not bring their four sons home now.
So what did it matter what the War Lord
said.

It was thoughts like these that they knew they had to conceal. It was because of thoughts like these that they did not trust themselves to go out and see other people, for they feared that by their looks if by nothing else, or by their silence or perhaps their tears, they might imply a blasphemy against the All Highest. And hunger made one so hasty. What might one not say? And so they stayed indoors.

But now. What would happen now? The War Lord was coming to Greinstein in order to hear the guns. One officer of the staff was to be billeted in their house. And what would happen now?

They talked the whole thing over. They must struggle and make an effort. The officer would be there for one evening. He would leave in the morning quite early in order to make things ready for the return to Potsdam: he had charge of the imperial car. So for one evening they must be merry. They would suppose, it was Herr

Schnitzelhaaser's suggestion, they would think all the evening that Belgium and France and Luxemburg all attacked the Fatherland, and that the Kaiser, utterly unprepared, quite unprepared, called on the Germans to defend their land against Belgium.

Yes, the old woman could imagine that; she could think it all the evening.

And then, — it was no use not being cheerful altogether, — then one must imagine a little more, just for the evening: it would come quite easy; one must think that the four boys were alive.

Hans too? (Hans was the youngest.)

Yes, all four. Just for the evening.

But if the officer asks?

He will not ask. What are four soldiers?

So it was all arranged; and at evening the officer came. He brought his own rations, so hunger came no nearer. Hunger just lay down outside the door and did not notice the officer.

At his supper the officer began to talk.

The Kaiser himself, he said, was at the Schartzhaus.

"So," said Herr Schnitzelhaaser; "just over the way." So close. Such an honour.

And indeed the shadow of the Schartz-haus darkened their garden in the morning.

It was such an honour, said Frau Schnitz-elhaaser too. And they began to praise the Kaiser. So great a War Lord, she said; the most glorious war there had ever been.

Of course, said the officer, it would end on the first of July.

Of course, said Frau Schnitzelhaaser. And so great an admiral, too. One must remember that also. And how fortunate we were to have him : one must not forget that. Had it not been for him the crafty Belgians would have attacked the Father-land, but they were struck down before they could do it. So much better to pre-vent a bad deed like that than merely to punish after. So wise. And had it not been for him, if it had not been for him . . .

The old man saw that she was breaking

down and hastily he took up that feverish praise. Feverish it was, for their hunger and bitter loss affected their minds no less than illness does, and the things they did they did hastily and intemperately. His praise of the War Lord raced on as the officer ate. He spoke of him as of those that benefit man, as of monarchs who bring happiness to their people. And now, he said, he is here in the Schartzhaus beside us, listening to the guns just like a common soldier.

Finally the guns, as he spoke, coughed beyond ominous hills. Contentedly the officer went on eating. He suspected nothing of the thoughts his host and hostess were hiding. At last he went upstairs to bed.

As fierce exertion is easy to the fevered, so they had spoken; and it wears them, so they were worn. The old woman wept when the officer went out of hearing. But old Herr Schnitzelhaaser picked up a big butcher's knife. "I will bear it no more," he said.

His wife watched him in silence as he went away with his knife. Out of the house he went and into the night. Through the open door she saw nothing; all was dark; even the Schartzhaus, where all was gay to-night, stood dark for fear of aëroplanes. The old woman waited in silence.

When Herr Schnitzelhaaser returned there was blood on his knife.

"What have you done?" the old woman asked him quite calmly. "I have killed our pig," he said.

She broke out then, all the more recklessly for the long restraint of the evening; the officer must have heard her.

"We are lost! We are lost!" she cried. "We may not kill our pig. Hunger has made you mad. You have ruined us."

"I will bear it no longer," he said. "I have killed our pig."

"But they will never let us eat it," she cried. "Oh, you have ruined us!"

"If you did not dare to kill our pig," he said, "why did you not stop me when you saw me go? You saw me go with the knife?"

"I thought," she said, "you were going to kill the Kaiser."

XXX

A DEED OF MERCY

AS Hindenburg and the Kaiser came down, as we read, from Mont d'Hiver, during the recent offensive, they saw on the edge of a crater two wounded British soldiers. The Kaiser ordered that they should be cared for: their wounds were bound up and they were given brandy, and brought round from unconsciousness. That is the German account of it, and it may well be true. It was a kindly act.

Probably had it not been for this the two men would have died among those desolate craters; no one would have known, and no one could have been blamed for it.

The contrast of this spark of imperial kindness against the gloom of the background of the war that the Kaiser made is a pleasant thing to see, even though it

illuminates for only a moment the savage
darkness in which our days are plunged.
It was a kindness that probably will long
be remembered to him. Even we, his
enemies, will remember it.   And who knows
but that when most he needs it his reward
for the act will be given him.

For Judas, they say, once in his youth,
gave his cloak, out of compassion, to a
shivering beggar, who sat shaken with ague,
in rags, in bitter need.   And the years went
by and Judas forgot his deed.   And long
after, in Hell, Judas they say was given one
day's respite at the end of every year because of this one kindness he had done so
long since in his youth.   And every year
he goes, they say, for a day and cools himself among the Arctic bergs; once every
year for century after century.

Perhaps some sailor on watch on a misty
evening blown far out of his course away to
the north saw something ghostly once on
an iceberg floating by, or heard some voice
in the dimness that seemed like the voice

of man, and came home with this weird story. And perhaps, as the story passed from lip to lip, men found enough justice in it to believe it true. So it came down the centuries.

Will seafarers ages hence on dim October evenings, or on nights when the moon is ominous through mist, red and huge and uncanny, see a lonely figure sometimes on the loneliest part of the sea, far north of where the *Lusitania* sank, gathering all the cold it can? Will they see it hugging a crag of iceberg wan as itself, helmet, cuirass and ice pale-blue in the mist together? Will it look towards them with ice-blue eyes through the mist, and will they question it, meeting on those bleak seas? Will it answer — or will the North Wind howl like voices? Will the cry of seals be heard, and ice floes grinding, and strange birds lost upon the wind that night, or will it speak to them in those distant years and tell them how it sinned, betraying man?

It will be a grim, dark story in that lonely

part of the sea, when he confesses to sailors, blown too far north, the dreadful thing he plotted against man. The date on which he is seen will be told from sailor to sailor. Queer taverns of distant harbours will know it well. Not many will care to be at sea that day, and few will risk being driven by stress of weather on the Kaiser's night to the bergs of the haunted part of sea.

And yet for all the grimness of the pale-blue phantom, with cuirass and helmet and eyes shimmering on deadly icebergs, and yet for all the sorrow of the wrong he did against man, the women drowned and the children, and all the good ships gone, yet will the horrified mariners meeting him in the mist grudge him no moment of the day he has earned, or the coolness he gains from the bergs, because of the kindness he did to the wounded men. For the mariners in their hearts are kindly men, and what a soul gains from kindness will seem to them well deserved.

XXXI

LAST SCENE OF ALL

AFTER John Calleron was hit he carried on in a kind of twilight of the mind. Things grew dimmer and calmer; harsh outlines of events became blurred; memories came to him; there was a singing in his ears like far-off bells. Things seemed more beautiful than they had a while ago; to him it was for all the world like evening after some quiet sunset, when lawns and shrubs and woods and some old spire look lovely in the late light, and one reflects on past days. Thus he carried on, seeing things dimly. And what is sometimes called "the roar of battle", those aërial voices that snarl and moan and whine and rage at soldiers, had grown dimmer too. It all seemed further away, and littler, as far things are. He still heard the bullets:

158

there is something so violently and intensely sharp in the snap of passing bullets at short ranges that you hear them in deepest thought, and even in dreams. He heard them, tearing by, above all things else. The rest seemed fainter and dimmer, and smaller and further away.

He did not think he was very badly hit, but nothing seemed to matter as it did a while ago. Yet he carried on.

And then he opened his eyes very wide and found he was back in London again in an underground train. He knew it at once by the look of it. He had made hundreds of journeys, long ago, by those trains. He knew by the dark, outside, that it had not yet left London; but what was odder than that, if one stopped to think of it, was that he knew exactly where it was going. It was the train that went away out into the country where he used to live as a boy. He was sure of that without thinking.

When he began to think how he came to be there he remembered the war as a very far-off thing. He supposed he had been unconscious a very long time. He was all right now.

Other people were sitting beside him on the same seat. They all seemed like people he remembered a very long time ago. In the darkness opposite, beyond the windows of the train, he could see their reflections clearly. He looked at the reflections but could not quite remember.

A woman was sitting on his left. She was quite young. She was more like some one that he most deeply remembered than all the others were. He gazed at her, and tried to clear his mind.

He did not turn and stare at her, but he quietly watched her reflection before him in the dark. Every detail of her dress, her young face, her hat, the little ornaments she wore, were minutely clear before him, looking out of the dark. So contented she looked you would say she was untouched by war.

As he gazed at the clear calm face and the dress that seemed neat though old and, like all things, so far away, his mind grew clearer and clearer. It seemed to him certain it was the face of his mother, but from thirty years ago, out of old memories and one picture. He felt sure it was his mother as she had been when he was very small. And yet after thirty years how could he know? He puzzled to try and be quite sure. But how she came to be there, looking like that, out of those oldest memories, he did not think of at all.

He seemed to be hugely tired by many things and did not want to think. Yet he was very happy, more happy even than tired men just come home all new to comfort.

He gazed and gazed at the face in the dark. And then he felt quite sure.

He was about to speak. Was she looking at him? Was she watching him, he wondered. He glanced for the first time to his own reflection in that clear row of faces.

His own reflection was not there, but blank dark showed between his two neighbours. And then he knew he was dead.

XXXII

OLD ENGLAND

TOWARDS winter's end on a high, big, bare down, in the south of England, John Plowman was ploughing. He was ploughing the brown field at the top of the hill, good soil of the clay; a few yards lower down was nothing but chalk, with shallow flinty soil and steep to plough; so they let briars grow there. For generations his forbears had ploughed on the top of that hill. John did not know how many. The hills were very old; it might have been always.

He scarcely looked to see if his furrow was going straight. The work he was doing was so much in his blood that he could almost feel if furrows were straight or not. Year after year they moved on the same old landmarks; thorn trees and briars mostly guided the plough, where they stood on the untamed land beyond; the thorn trees grew old at their guiding, and still the furrows varied not by the breadth of a hoof-mark.

John, as he ploughed, had leisure to meditate on much besides the crops; he knew so much of the crops that his thoughts could easily run free from them; he used to meditate on who they were that lived in briar and thorn tree, and danced as folk said all through midsummer night, and sometimes blessed and sometimes harmed the crops; for he knew that in Old England were wonderful ancient things, odder and older things than many folks knew. And his eyes had leisure to see much beside the furrows, for he could almost feel the furrows going straight.

One day at his ploughing, as he watched the thorn ahead, he saw the whole big hill besides, looking south, and the lands below it; one day he saw in the bright sun of late winter a horseman riding the road through the wide lands below. The horseman shone as he rode, and wore white linen over what was shining, and on the linen was a big red cross. "One of them knights," John Plowman said to himself or his horse, "going to them crusades." And he went on with his ploughing all that day satisfied, and remembered what he had seen for years, and told his son.

For there is in England, and there always was, mixed with the needful things that feed or shelter the race, the wanderer-feeling for romantic causes that runs deep and strange through the other thoughts, as the Gulf Stream runs through the sea. Sometimes generations of John Plowman's family would go by and no high romantic cause would come to sate that feeling. They would work on just the same though a little sombrely, as though some good thing had been grudged them. And then the Crusades had come, and John Plowman had seen the Red Cross knight go by, riding towards the sea in the morning, and John Plowman was satisfied.

Some generations later a man of the same
name was ploughing the same hill. They
still ploughed the brown clay at the top and
left the slope wild, though there were many
changes. And the furrows were wonderfully straight still. And half he watched a
thorn tree ahead as he ploughed and half
he took in the whole hill sloping south and
the wide lands below it, far beyond which
was the sea. They had a railway now down
in the valley. The sunlight glittering near
the end of winter shone on a train that was
marked with great white squares and red
crosses on them.

John Plowman stopped his horses and
looked at the train. "An ambulance
train," he said, "coming up from the coast."
He thought of the lads he knew and wondered if any were there. He pitied the men
in that train and envied them. And then
there came to him the thought of England's
cause and of how those men had upheld it,
at sea and in crumbling cities. He thought
of the battle whose echoes reached some-

times to that field, whispering to furrows and thorn trees that had never heard them before. He thought of the accursed tyrant's cruel might, and of the lads that had faced it. He saw the romantic splendour of England's cause. He was old but had seen the glamour for which each generation looked. Satisfied in his heart and cheered with a new content he went on with his age-old task in the business of man with the hills.